"Gavin O'Neal was your husband?"

Kyle shook his head dazedly. "He was a legend in the business world. You were going to marry Kenny after being with a man like that?"

"For a time I thought I loved Kenny," Shelby said. "And I only marry for love."

"And what do you go to bed for? Pleasure?" Kyle rasped. "Well, this has just stopped being that. I'm no more willing to be a rich widow's plaything than Kenny was once he came to his senses."

"Kenny's decision had nothing to do with sense," Shelby flared. "And if by some miracle he should actually tell you the truth, don't come back to me with apologies!"

Last night had been an illusion—a beautiful one—and that was all she wanted to remember.

Books by Carole Mortimer

HARLEQUIN PRESENTS

These books may be available at your local bookseller.

Don't miss any of our special offers. Write to us at the following address for information on our newest releases.

Harlequin Reader Service
P.O. Box 52040, Phoenix, AZ 85072-2040
Canadian address: P.O. Box 2800, Postal Station A,
5170 Yonge St., Willowdale, Ont. M2N 6J3

CAROLE MORTIMER

the passionate lover

Harlequin Books

TORONTO • NEW YORK • LONDON
AMSTERDAM • PARIS • SYDNEY • HAMBURG
STOCKHOLM • ATHENS • TOKYO • MILAN

For
John and Matthew

———————◆———————

Harlequin Presents first edition May 1985
ISBN 0-373-10786-2

Original hardcover edition published in 1985
by Mills & Boon Limited

CHAPTER ONE

THE heavy snow beat with icy determination against her numbed cheeks as she stumbled through its blinding thickness, the fashionable black anorak she wore no defence against its relentlessness. Kenny had written and warned her that the Montana winters could be harshly cold, but she had knowingly thought only of the icy English winters she had known all her life, little dreaming that when Kenny said harsh he meant so cold the snow had turned to stinging icicles before it even reached the ground. Consequently the fleecy anorak and fashionably tight denims tucked into high-heeled boots were little protection against the blizzard she suddenly found herself in.

And it was a blizzard. She may never have experienced one before but she knew she was in the midst of one now. The snow was already feet deep in places, and as it fell fast and furious against her face and body it gave no indication of stopping for some time, the dryness of the minus-thirty temperature taking her breath away as she fought her way slowly forward.

She wasn't even sure how she had come to wander off in this way, had been sure, when she first realised she could no longer see the blue four-wheel-drive truck, that Kenny would find her within minutes. But more than minutes had passed now; she seemed to have been wandering around for hours. And she wasn't even sure she was going in the right direction!

She could even be walking around in hideously lost circles.

She took a firm grip on herself at that thought. Kenny would find her any second now. He had to!

She couldn't help thinking how different the life she had lived here the last two weeks was from the one she had made for herself in London during and since her marriage to Gavin. Shelby O'Neal, one of London's most successful and exclusive hostesses living on a ranch in Montana, even seriously planning to marry one of the Double K's owners. The first part of the Double K she was sure she loved, the second part ...! Kyle Whitney, Kenny's older cousin, was someone she preferred not to think about.

But as the slow, painful minutes passed and she still stumbled through the blinding blizzard in the fast darkening night one thought possessed and held her horror-struck brain. She was going to die out here in this frozen wasteland!

Her legs felt so tired as she struggled to stay upright in the deep snow, and she could no longer feel her toes in the leather boots, the hard snow that fell against the sensitive skin of her face now feeling like painful needles digging into her. She wasn't winning this fight, and although not normally a defeatist she knew she couldn't fight and win this battle against such fierce elements. She was going to die, out here alone in the snow, was just going to collapse and die of the cold and no one would even know it had happened. For a wild hysterical moment she wondered if anyone would care! Then she berated herself. Kenny would care, they were to be married in a few weeks' time. Then why hadn't he found her, damn him?

She was being unfair now. But this whole situation was unfair. The tears dried on her cheeks before they barely had time to fall, and she wiped at her face impatiently. Twenty-five was too young to die, especially when she had so much to live for. If it wouldn't be so damned futile in this howling wind she would scream— Scream . . .! Why not? It was a sure fact that Kenny wouldn't be able to see her in this, but there was a chance, just a chance, that he might hear her if she screamed.

Shelby knew it was hopeless even as she opened her mouth to emit the cry for help. The words seemed to be thrown back at her as the wind whipped eerily about her, and she knew that the sound of her voice had just added brief depth to the wind before it was swallowed up. It *was* futile, she was being a fool to tell herself any differently. No one could find her in this weather, she could be miles from where she and Kenny had got out of the truck to admire the beautiful scenery of the snow-covered mountains, the snowfall only light then, or she could, alternatively, be only feet away and just unable to see him.

Whatever, she was too tired to care any more. She had never felt so tired and utterly helpless in her life before, just wanted to lie down and sleep until it was all over. The crisp white snow suddenly looked like an inviting bed of floating clouds, warm and inviting, like the arms of a lover.

And maybe she would have laid down in his arms and slept forever if she hadn't found the cabin.

To say she found the cabin wasn't strictly true, it found her. Actually she walked into it. Her visibility was down to nil by this time, her body one long ache, and when she walked into the solid object in front of her she assumed it was just another of the tall pine trees she had managed to avoid as they suddenly loomed up in front of her in her haphazard walk. The blow she received to her temple as she made contact made her head ring, and she fell to her knees in numbed pain and despair, sure she wasn't going to be able to get up again. Then she realised the object that had caused her so much pain was too big to be a mere tree, the shape of the wood seeming to indicate the tree lay horizontal rather than vertical. She almost had herself convinced she was hallucinating when in her stumbling her hand suddenly encountered a door handle and she actually fell inside the cabin.

It was very dark inside, too dark to see if it had any occupants, and Shelby looked into the gloom warily. She may have got herself into a worse situation than before! 'Er—Hello?' Her voice came out quivering with uncertainty, all of the self-confidence she possessed as the owner of O'Neal's, a women's salon in London, seeming to have deserted her in the face of this previously unthinkable danger.

When she realised there was going to be no reply to her tentative query, not even a stirring of movement inside, she knew there was no occupant, her breath leaving her with a relieved sigh. A sigh that was quickly followed by deep-rooted panic. If there was no occupant of the cabin then she was still alone, with no way of knowing where she was or if she would ever get out of here alive.

But at least she was alive now, and with shelter from the harshness of the wind and snow she could remain that way for a time. Perhaps there would even be the makings of a fire to keep her warm tonight, and tomorrow—Tomorrow Kenny would find her, she was sure of it.

She stumbled inside, closing the door—and the icy cold wind—behind her. It was dark inside, so dark she couldn't make out her surroundings at all. God, if only she smoked, then she would at least have had a lighter or matches in the pocket of the jacket that had so far proved useless. But she didn't smoke, and so consequently she didn't have any matches, only an instinct that told her the fireplace would be directly across from the door if there were one. And surely any self-respecting owner of such a remote cabin would leave matches on the mantelshelf? It was all she could hope for.

The cabin proved to be wider across than she had imagined, although the fireplace was there, and miraculously, so were the matches! Her hands trembled as she ripped off her gloves and struck one of the precious matches, looking around in wonder at the well-stocked and provisioned cabin. Whoever it belonged to couldn't be that far away, possibly just in the nearest town for a few days' shopping and seeing friends. Whoever he was she felt grateful to him, would leave a note of explanation and reimbursement for anything she used.

One thing she had discovered on that cursory look around the cabin were some old-fashioned oil-lamps, and she lit one of them with her next match, grateful for its cheering warmth as she took stock of her surroundings. There was certainly no luxury to be found here, but there was the fireplace that would soon warm her, and a wood-burning stove that she would be able to use to heat up food and water on. She had never camped out in her life, never stayed anywhere this primitive before, but she had a feeling she was going to be plunged in at the deep-end, that she had to learn, and quickly, if she were to survive. It wasn't even night yet, only early evening, and the temperature that was already more severe than anything she had ever known before could get even lower during the night hours, making her first priority the lighting of a fire.

She was sure it wasn't the best fire anyone had ever built, and the stove threw more smoke out into the room at first than went up the chimney, but she soon fixed that by adjusting the door so that it fit into place better, and the fire threw out enough heat for her to be able to remove her jacket and take stock of the rest of the room.

For the cabin was only one room, well-planned to give the maximum amount of space, but still only one room for eating, sitting and sleeping. Four bunk beds, two on each side of the room, one above the other, stood at one end, a small sitting and eating area in the middle, and the wood-burning stove at the other end to cook on. But the furniture looked clean and serviceable, the scatter-rugs on the floor giving it a homely touch. Rustic charm, her London friends would have said it had, although they would have expected plumbing and electricity to go along with that charm. Shelby was sure it didn't have the latter, and it didn't seem to have plumbing either. But at least she was safe from the blizzard, the inevitability of dying fading as the warmth increased in the room.

Quite when the noises outside began to bother her she didn't know, but halfway through drinking the soup she had heated she suddenly had the impulse to lock and bolt the door. The noises were only the ones of the storm, she knew that, the wind and the swaying creak of the surrounding trees, and yet the feeling persisted, so much so that in the end she did lock and bolt the door just to settle her own mind. It wasn't just the human factor that frightened her, it was the wildlife too. A Londoner born and raised, she hadn't even seen a real live cow until she was ten years old, and then only because the school had taken them on a trip to a farm for the day. Kenny had told her they had deer and other small harmless animals in the thousands of acres of valley and mountains that was the Double K ranch, but she hadn't thought to ask if they had bears too.

Every noise outside now seemed to take on frightening proportions, and she jumped nervously as a branch of a tree crashed against the window. But was it a tree? It could be a bear, or a wolf! She had read books and seen films where people had gone insane as a creature of the night stood watch outside cabins like this.

Was that what she was doing? Surely she was made of sterner stuff than that? She had lived through, and survived so much the last few years, surely she was strong enough not to crack up at the sound of natural forest noises?

But were they natural? She could have sworn she heard something moving about outside just now, and not just the random noises of the wind and trees but a definite pattern around the cabin. Her hands tightened about the mug that contained her soup, her eyes wide with fear as she looked towards the door expectantly.

The first rattle of the door frightened her so

much the mug of soup dropped out of her hand, and she stood up to back against the wall as it rattled once again, an eerie sound, much like a growl, accompanying it this time. God, there was a wild animal out there, and it sounded as if it were going to break in at any moment!

Shelby had never been so terrified, listening as the predator moved away from the door to circle the cabin once more. Her heart rose in her throat as she saw the furry face at the window, her breathing seeming to stop altogether as a hairy paw struck the window pane, the eerie growl accompanying the fierce tapping movement.

The window! God, she had locked and bolted the door and forgotten to shutter the windows! As she hurried to do so the face appeared at the window again, and she stepped back with a scream, her hands shaking so badly now she was incapable of closing the shutters even if she had wanted to. She watched the door with horrified fascination as the creature outside began to pound against the wood, sure that the bolts and lock would give at any moment, splinters already starting to break away from the top bolt.

She huddled down in the corner of the farthest bunk bed. Suddenly there was an ear-splitting splintering of wood, and the door banged open with such ferocity Shelby couldn't hold back her gasp of horror and fear.

Heavy fur framed the aggressive face, cold grey eyes turned on her in total assessment. 'Why the hell didn't you open the goddamned door?' Kyle Whitney grated in harsh condemnation, throwing back the furred hood of his thick jacket to reveal his overlong dark hair, snow-coated at the front of it.

Shelby only had time to recognise him before

the faintness became a black fog and she fell backwards on the bed in total collapse, still unsure whether her unexpected visitor was a predator or friend. . .

She was still lying on the bunk bed when she woke up, although she had been moved into a more comfortable position, a heavy down quilt placed on top of her to keep her warm.

Her panicked gaze flew across the room, hardly daring to move as she once again recognised the harshly glowering profile of Kyle Whitney as he stared into the flames of the roaring fire. He looked more human now, the heavy jacket removed, the frozen snow that had clung to his face and hair now melted, leaving his hair curling damply against his forehead and ears, hair that although carelessly styled grew overlong to the dark sweater he wore. He was drinking what smelt like coffee, his narrow-eyed attention fixed sightlessly on the fire as he took huge swallows of the warming brew. He looked hard and un-approachable, much as he had the first time she had seen him two weeks ago.

She had met Kenny Whitney in London six months ago, an accidental meeting when he had called to collect one of the girls who worked in the salon. He had come back to the salon many times after that first meeting, but to see Shelby now, and not Anne. The other girl accepted the loss of his attention with shrugging nonchalance, quickly finding herself another companion. Shelby found it less easy to adapt to this change of affections, refusing all Kenny's invitations with a cool disdain she hoped would quickly dissuade him. It hadn't. His pursuit of her had been relentless and persistent, so much so that after she had watched him stand outside her flat in the rain for over an hour one evening she had finally relented and invited him in.

He had stayed several hours that evening, the two of them discussing everything and nothing, Shelby finding his life that was so different from her own very interesting, Kenny in London on a year's agricultural course, his cousin and partner back in Montana running the ranch in his absence. Kenny's life was everything she had ever read life on a ranch could be, and he was everything she would have expected a modern-day cowboy to be, rugged, tough, and very decisive. So decisive, in fact, that when he asked her to see him again she found herself agreeing, her earlier reluctance forgotten under the warmth of his slow charm.

The next two months had been the happiest she had known for a long time, Kenny insisting they meet whenever they could, his passionate but undemanding loving just what she needed to make her respond to him as she had to no man since Gavin.

And then the two months had ended, and with it Kenny's time in England, his presence now needed back in Montana. Shelby had done her best to hide her disappointment, knowing she was going to miss him. Nevertheless, she was surprised when he asked her to go back to Montana with him. She hadn't accepted him, of course. It was only a year since she had lost Gavin, another serious relationship was out of the question just yet.

But Kenny had been persistent, even from a distance, writing to her constantly, always repeating his offer for her to go out to Montana, pleading with her almost. Until finally she had agreed.

She had been aware of Kyle Whitney's disapproval of her from the moment Kenny had brought her back to the ranch from the airport. It wasn't that the older man was actually rude, but his contemptuous amusement whenever he spoke to her was enough to let her know he didn't like her and saw no reason to make an effort to be polite to her.

But if Kyle Whitney didn't like or approve of her he came as something of a shock to her too. She had assumed he would be in his early or mid-twenties, as Kenny was, instead he was in his mid-thirties, hard and cynical, seeming to view everyone and everything through a jaundiced eye. He was also one of the most handsome men she had ever seen, his body lean and muscular in the faded denims and thick shirts he usually wore, his hair almost black although run through with strands of grey, dark brows over piercingly light grey eyes, a hawklike nose, and a mouth that looked as if it should have had a sensual curve to it, but which was habitually set in a thin straight line of disapproval.

It was set that way now as he continued to look into the fire, and after the way he had verbally attacked her after forcefully entering the cabin she was loath to remind him of her presence, the door bearing evidence of having been repaired, something he would have had little patience with.

But as if becoming aware of being watched he suddenly turned in her direction, his eyes narrowing in steely acknowledgement as he saw her looking at him in return. He stood up slowly, moving with the natural grace she had come to associate with him. 'Coffee?' he questioned with the minimum of effort she had also learnt was usual for him.

She sat up, forgetting any idea she might have had of pretending she was still asleep. 'Please,' she nodded acceptance, moving to sit in one of the two chairs placed either side of the fireplace as he handed her a steaming mug of coffee. She drank it thirstily, needing its warmth despite the heat that now permeated the room from the roaring fire.

Kyle still stood over her, dark and threatening. 'Perhaps now you wouldn't mind answering the question I asked you a short time ago, namely why I had to break my way in here?' he drawled with disdain.

Shelby couldn't prevent the hot colour that flooded her cheeks, mumbling into her coffee mug.

'What did you say?' he bit out impatiently.

She looked up at him with blazing green eyes, her reddish-gold hair falling just below her shoulders in silky waves as she bent her head back. 'I thought you were an animal of some kind,' she repeated resentfully.

His mouth twisted. 'What kind?'

She sighed. 'A wolf, or a—a bear. I just didn't know!' she added irritably as he began to smile, a smile full of that contemptuous amusement he viewed her with.

'We don't have either in this part of Montana,' he told her dryly.

'Well I wasn't to know that!' she snapped.

'Lady, you're a walking disaster,' he lowered his long length into the chair opposite her. 'You wandered off to God knows where thinking you could be eaten alive! What are you, stupid, or just plain dumb?'

'Neither!' she flashed at his derogatory attitude. 'I didn't let you in, did I?'

'No,' he acknowledged ruefully. 'But if I had been a bear, perhaps a hungry grizzly, maybe I would have found you delectable enough a morsel to stick a paw through the window and drag you outside.'

Shelby repressed the shiver of revulsion and fear as he put into words what had been going through her mind only minutes earlier, knowing he wanted to frighten her. 'I just forgot to put the shutters up——'

'They wouldn't have stopped a hungry grizzly.'

'Then why bother to have them?' she snapped, noticing they were shut now.

'To keep the warmth in and the cold out,' he mocked her stupidity.

So that was the reason for the added warmth in the room. She had a feeling this man was always right, that he was never made to feel the fool that she was now. 'How did you find me?'

'With extreme difficulty!' he rasped grimly.

Too late she realised her change of subject was even more inflammatory than the original one. Damn the man, couldn't he see she had had a scare? Kenny would have been comforting her by now instead of berating her in this way. 'I'm sorry,' she muttered, resentful of his coldness.

Kyle looked unimpressed with her apology. 'I've had a dozen men out looking for you ever since Kenny came back to the house and told us what had happened,' he bit out. 'I hope to God they've all had sense enough to go back home!'

She could see that he had a right to be angry with her, although she hadn't deliberately set out to get lost. She couldn't help wishing it had been one of the other dozen men who had been the one to find her! 'I didn't need you to come looking for me,' she told him quietly. 'I could have found my way once the blizzard calmed down.'

Contemptuous grey eyes raked over her mercilessly. 'Could you really?'

'Yes!' Her eyes flashed again.

He gave her a look that spoke volumes. 'And just when do you expect the blizzard to stop?'

'I don't know,' she shrugged. 'But I'm sure I could have managed until it did——'

'You didn't even know where the water supply was!'

'I——'

'Did you?' he rasped forcefully.

She had been wondering where he got the water to make the coffee, but she was too proud now to tell him so. 'I can melt snow as easily as you did——'

'Always supposing you got up enough courage to open the door,' he cut in again with cold derision. 'And I didn't melt the snow. There's a sink over there——'

'But no taps,' she said hastily. 'I've already looked.'

'There's a lever just above it,' he told her in a calm voice. 'It will give you all the water you need. It's pumped up from an underground stream.'

'You seem to know this cabin very well,' Shelby snapped her resentment of his contempt.

'I should do,' he drawled. 'It's on Double K land.'

She should have realised that! She had got lost on Double K land, so it stood to reason, with the thousands of acres they owned, that she hadn't wandered off it. She felt even more foolish than ever. 'What is this place?'

'My men use it during branding, it saves time

if they don't have to ride out each day,' he explained with barely concealed impatience for her naïveté.

She resented his use of the word 'my' men, knew that he and Kenny were joint owners of the ranch. Although Kenny didn't seem to mind that his cousin gave most of the orders, had probably learnt from experience that Kyle was a man who simply didn't take or obey orders from anyone.

'When can we get out of here?' she asked abruptly.

He shrugged, very relaxed as he leant back in his chair. 'Your guess is as good as mine.'

Shelby gave him a sharp look. 'What do you mean?'

He tilted his head towards the door. 'Hear that?' he quirked dark brows.

'The wind?' she frowned.

'The wind,' he nodded mockingly. 'The weather report forecast it will continue all night, possibly during tomorrow too.' He gave her a meaningful look. 'And while the wind keeps howling we keep sitting here.'

Shelby had gone very pale, swallowing hard. 'You mean we could be—be snowed in here?'

'I mean we already are snowed in here. Even if another drop of snow doesn't fall we're still stuck.'

'There's no need to be sarcastic——'

'There's every need, damn you!' Suddenly the relaxed pose had gone, to be replaced by a man full of fury, a fury that made his eyes glitter dangerously. 'I don't have the time to spare to come chasing after a stupid idiot like you, let alone spend days out here baby-sitting!'

'*Baby-sitting!*'

'You heard me,' he rasped. 'You have no idea how to fend for yourself——'

'It isn't exactly a wilderness!'

'No?' He stood up, pulling her roughly to her feet, his calloused hand digging painfully into her nape as he dragged her over to the window to throw back the shutters. 'Look out there,' he ordered through gritted teeth. 'And tell me what it is if it isn't a wilderness.'

She wanted to protest that he had no right to treat her this way, that even if he didn't like her he could at least treat her with a little respect. But the sight that met her eyes silenced any protests she might have made over his rough handling. Although the wind still raged the snow had stopped falling, and every way that she looked a deep white blanket stretched into the distance, no familiar landmarks in sight, just snow and more snow wherever she looked.

'I had no idea . . .' she breathed softly, in awe of the terrifying beauty outside.

'Of course you didn't,' he scorned, releasing her to resecure the shutters. 'Like I said, you're a complete novice when it comes to surviving in conditions like this.'

Once again his contempt angered her. 'And I suppose you're an old hand at it?' she challenged recklessly.

Kyle folded muscled arms across his broad chest. 'Let's put it this way,' he drawled. 'Which one of us, do you think, has the most chance of surviving out here alone?'

She flushed at his taunt. 'That's an unfair question, you were born here——'

'Exactly,' he nodded grimly. 'So why don't you just bow to the inevitable and let me make the decisions from now on?'

'That's something you're good at, isn't it?' she was stung into retorting, not used to being treated as if she had less intelligence than a child. 'Kyle Whitney gives the orders and everyone jumps to obey.'

His eyes narrowed to steely slits. 'And that bothers you?'

'No, it doesn't *bother* me,' she flushed. 'I just don't intend being another of the yes-men you surround yourself with——'

'Or women,' he drawled mockingly.

'Or women,' she snapped irritably. 'You chose to come looking for me, I didn't ask you to.'

'Your sort never asks for anything, Mrs O'Neal,' he bit out contemptuously. 'But they take readily enough when something is offered to them.'

Shelby stiffened at his intended insult. 'What are you implying I've "taken"?'

'Kenny sent you the airline ticket to come out here, didn't he?' Kyle reminded scathingly.

The plane ticket had been in Kenny's letter immediately after he had received her letter telling him she would go out for a visit. It hadn't been something she had asked for or needed, well able to pay her own airfare. But she had seen it as a gesture of Kenny's love. She certainly hadn't thought anyone would view her as a money-grasping mercenary because of it. Kyle Whitney didn't know how wrong he was!

'You're wrong about me, Mr Whitney——'

'Am I?' he derided harshly. 'I don't think so. You're a young and attractive widow, and you came out here thinking Kenny would be a gullible meal-ticket.'

'No——'

'Oh yes,' he insisted coldly, his mouth turned

back in a sneer. 'When Kenny came back from England extolling the virtues of a beautiful widow I had some misgivings. When he dropped the girl he had been dating since high school because of you I knew I was right to be worried. But I thought time and distance would dull his memory of you, that he would soon get over the infatuation. But you didn't intend for him to do that, did you. Oh no, you wrote to him almost every day——'

'Twice a week,' she defended indignantly.

The coldness of his gaze scorned her. 'Whatever. It was enough to ensure that he didn't forget you, and that's the point I'm trying to make.'

Shelby had never been subjected to such injustice in her life before. Kyle Whitney didn't know the first thing about her, and yet he presumed to be her judge and jury on the insubstantial evidence he had picked up here and there about her. 'Kenny is hardly a child that you need to——'

'He's two years younger than you are.'

She hadn't forgotten that fact; it had been one of the reasons she had been reluctant to become involved with him in the first place. But he had easily over-ruled that objection, and once she got to know him she hadn't really thought the two years mattered either. But as far as Kyle Whitney was concerned it was just another black mark against her. And his condemnation was unfair. Kenny had finished with his childhood sweetheart before leaving for London the previous year, and if his cousin didn't know that then it wasn't her fault, Kenny certainly didn't have to tell the older man everything. And she may have written to Kenny twice a week, but he had written much

more than that, more like the every day Kyle
Whitney had accused her of doing.

'—although thank God he seems to have gotten
over that now,' Kyle rasped.

Shelby suddenly realised she had been so deep
in thought she had missed this last scathing
comment. 'Sorry?' she prompted with a frown.

'You might well look concerned.' The ghost of
a smile creased the hard face.

He was a man who smiled little, she had learnt
that over the last few weeks. The only time he
seemed to relax was when he was out working
with the men on the ranch. 'Could you explain
what you just said?' She still frowned, puzzled by
what he was trying to tell her.

He shrugged his broad shoulders. 'Doesn't the
fact that Kenny isn't one of the people out
looking for you speak for itself?' he drawled.

Shelby felt her heart give an uncomfortable
lurch, watching Kyle with disbelieving eyes as he
poured himself another mug of the strong coffee,
almost as if he hadn't just dealt her a terrible
blow emotionally. 'Is he hurt in some way?' she
demanded, concerned.

Even white teeth gleamed against the mahogany
skin as Kyle gave another brief, humourless
smile. 'I guess after the way he's been running
around after you since you got here it must be
pretty difficult for you to accept or understand
that he just didn't want to look for you.'

'Why?' she asked through stiff lips, knowing
that no matter how much this man may dislike
her, he wouldn't lie to get her out of Kenny's life.
But if what he was saying was true ...!

Kyle sipped the coffee. 'The argument you
had must have been really something,' he
looked at her admiringly. 'Or maybe he was

just too disgusted after the way you walked off like that.'

'But I——'

'It was a damn fool thing to do,' he growled, the harshness back. 'Even if you were mad at Kenny.'

'But——'

'And when we get out of here I'll give you the hiding you deserve for doing it,' he added grimly. 'You might not have been found until the spring.'

Shelby gave up all effort of trying to defend herself. 'The spring?' she echoed dazedly.

He looked at her steadily. 'When the thaw comes.'

She felt herself blanch as his meaning became clear. Although she was also concerned as to how he had got the impression she and Kenny had argued; it simply wasn't true. And yet he said Kenny hadn't helped look for her. She didn't understand any of this.

CHAPTER TWO

'MR Whitney——'

'I believe Kenny decided days ago it was to be Kyle,' he rasped dismissively, moving with that minimum of movement that was so natural to him. 'Now are you capable of helping me get us something for dinner? If not perhaps you could find some cutlery to put on the table.' He was already engrossed in the contents of the tins in the cupboards over and under the sink.

'I can cook, Kyle——' She snapped her resentment at his assumption that she didn't know one end of a kitchen from the other.

'Thank God for small mercies.' He gave her a look that implied he thought she was good for little else.

Shelby was well aware of how she must appear to him. A little over five feet in height, with gleaming red-gold hair just past her shoulders, a beautiful face dominated by thickly lashed green eyes, her slender figure shown to perfection in the dark green cashmere sweater and tightly fitting denims, he must be cursing the day she had walked into his life, must wish he hadn't come looking for her either!

'Kyle, about Kenny——'

'He was on his way to see Wendy when I last saw him,' he dismissed with cruel honesty.

Wendy Seymore was Kenny's old childhood sweetheart, Shelby knew that, she had even met the other girl on one occasion, an embarrassingly awkward time when Wendy had made no secret of her dislike of Shelby. In the circumstances she hadn't been able to blame the other girl, but she found it hard to believe that Kenny had left her out in the blizzard while he went to visit the other girl on her father's neighbouring ranch. It didn't sound like the Kenny she knew and loved. There had to be a logical explanation for his behaviour. If only she could think of one!

'Look at this practically, Shelby.' Surprisingly Kyle's voice had softened a little as he noticed her pained preoccupation. 'You've had a free two-week holiday in Montana. It's more return than a lot of women get.'

Her mouth firmed. 'If you're implying what I think you are, Mr Whitney,' the formality seemed perfectly fitting in the circumstances! 'I can assure you that I haven't been paid for services rendered!' Two angry spots of colour darkened her cheeks.

His calculating gaze moved over her with slow thoroughness, from the tip of her gleaming head to the boots on her feet, his eyes darkening as they encountered the latter. 'You should have taken those off,' he bit out accusingly. 'They're wet through! I bet your denims are too,' he added questioningly. 'It's a little difficult to tell when they already fit so—snugly,' he said derisively.

She knew the disparaging comment was warranted, but when she had done her shopping for this trip back in London these clothes had seemed ideal for the climate while still remaining feminine. She had only realised the absurdity of them when the denims were too tight for her to sit astride the horse Kenny had persuaded her to ride, the boots too high-heeled for her to walk with any degree of composure over the uneven ground of the Double K yards.

But Kyle was right about the denims being damp, the snow having been up to her thighs in places. Although what he expected her to do about the situation she didn't know. He must be as wet as she was, and neither of them had a change of clothes available. He soon had an answer to that!

'I suggest you take off your clothes before you catch pneumonia,' he continued at her silence.

'Certainly not!'

'And wrap up in a blanket until they dry,' he added over her outraged comment.

'There aren't any blankets,' she told him with almost triumphant spite.

With a pitying glance in her direction he moved to the chests that stood beneath the two lower bunks, pulling them out to display more quilts like the one he had placed over her earlier, and also blankets and sheets, enough for all four of the bunk beds.

'Help yourself,' he stood up. 'But for God's sake hurry up and get out of those wet clothes.'

'You're as wet as I am!' The way his own denims clung to the lean length of his muscular legs hadn't escaped her notice.

'And I intend doing something about it as soon as I have you sorted out.'

'I'm not a child——'

'Then quit acting like one!' he suddenly exploded with temper, running one lean hand through the thickness of his dark hair. 'Look, we're both tired, after being out in that how could we be anything else! I for one am too tired to argue with you about something as trivial as wet clothing. I'm also hungry, and when I'm hungry my temper gets frayed.'

'You can say that again!' she snapped,

wishing he would stop talking down to her all the time.

'And, obviously, so does yours,' he added with pointed sarcasm.

She had the grace to look abashed. 'I am a little damp,' she admitted softly. 'Hungry too.'

'Then the sooner you undress the sooner we can eat,' Kyle wasn't prepared to give an inch. 'I'll make up the fire, you can change here,' he added impatiently as she made no effort to move while he stood there watching her, striding across the room to begin throwing logs on the fire, his back firmly turned towards her, rigid with displeasure.

'Er——'

'What is it now?' His impatience was coming to boiling point as he turned to glare at her.

'The bathroom,' she explained reluctantly, embarrassed at having to ask him about something so personal.

'There isn't one,' he derided.

'I know that,' she flushed as he deliberately misunderstood her. God, she wasn't stupid enough to think there would actually be a *bath*room out here! 'I don't want a bath, I'm asking where the——'

'It's outside,' he finally took pity on her discomfort. 'At the side of the cabin. This place wasn't built to be used as a winter home,' he told her without apology for the fact that she had to go out in the cold once again. 'It's used for a few weeks in the spring and summer, there's no reason to have the bathroom inside. The food is kept in stock here just in case,' he added grimly.

'In case some irresponsible woman goes and gets herself lost,' Shelby finished tersely, knowing that was what he had been implying.

'Exactly,' he nodded abruptly. 'Take one of the lamps with you,' he instructed. 'I'd hate you to wander off and get lost again.'

She bit back the angry retort that hovered on the edge of her lips, knowing that anything she had to say would only give him the opportunity to make yet another blistering condemnation of her. Besides, her very real need for the bathroom was more important at the moment, and after pulling on her hat, jacket and gloves she picked up the lamp to leave.

'It's to the right,' Kyle suddenly told her, when he had appeared to be taking no notice of her.

Shelby flashed him a grateful look, almost knocked back inside by the freezing cold wind that hit her as soon as she opened the door. The snow may have stopped falling for the moment but the wind howled on like a demented demon, driving her back as she fought her way to the small wooden building next to the cabin. By the time she had battled her way there and then back again she was beginning to wonder if it was worth it, feeling more exhausted than ever.

Kyle was still sitting where she had left him when she turned from forcing the door closed, although he frowned as he looked up at her. 'Did you fall?' he rasped, standing up.

The way he was moving towards her made her back up against the door, her eyes wide.

'For God's sake,' he bit out harshly. 'I'm not so desperate that I would resort to forcing myself on a woman who, at the moment, resembles the attractions of a drowned rat!' His eyes glittered dangerously. 'You have a cut on your head, I merely wanted to take a look at it.'

Shelby felt very young and very stupid at that

moment. Which was ridiculous! She was a very capable and successful busineswoman in London, her age and widowed status precluding her being young. But she would be the first to admit that she was out of her element in this situation, that although she disliked Kyle Whitney intensely, hated the way he constantly reminded her how stupid she had been to get lost in the way that she had, she was very grateful that he was here. But she knew he didn't feel the same way, that he didn't find her in the least attractive, as she didn't him, but her nerves were at such a taut pitch her recoil from him had been instinctive rather than intentional.

'I'm sorry,' she muttered as he examined her right temple with surprisingly gentle fingers. 'And I think I probably got that when I fell into the cabin earlier.'

His mouth twisted with derision where it was on a level with her eyes, but the scathing comment she had been expecting didn't come. Instead he concentrated on the cut. 'It doesn't look too bad, although the skin is broken. I'll clean it up for you once you have those wet clothes off.' He stepped back.

She hadn't realised just how close he was standing until the warmth of his body was removed, feeling a sudden shiver through her body. 'Get undressed,' Kyle mistook the shiver for one of cold, turning back to the fire to give her what privacy he could in the close confines of the cabin.

Her clothes clung to her damply as she peeled them off, making the task doubly difficult, the cold seeming to have seeped into her very bones, the blanket she wrapped around her sarong-wise saving her modesty but giving little real warmth.

It was also rough and abrasive against her skin. And she didn't even have a brush for her hair. Reaction suddenly began to set in, and she sat down heavily on one of the beds as the tears cascaded down her cheeks.

Everything had seemed so wonderful until today. She couldn't have been happier, was marrying the man she loved; Kenny had even decided they should live in London after the wedding, dispelling her worries about the salon. Now she had got lost in the snow, had been told Kenny no longer wanted to marry her, and was stranded in a primitive cabin with no clothes but what she had been wearing, with a man who made no attempt to hide the fact that he despised her.

It was all too much, too sudden, and the tears fell unchecked, the sound of her sobbing finally causing Kyle to turn and look at her. 'What the——!' He was across the room in two strides, sitting down beside her on the bed, pulling her into his arms, her face buried against his chest. 'What is it, Shelby?' he asked gruffly. 'Tell me what's wrong?'

The man must be an insensitive clod if he didn't know. 'Everything,' she sniffed miserably.

'Hey, we'll be all right. We'll be out of here in a few days, and then——'

'A few days!' she wailed, crying harder than ever.

'I'll see that you don't starve.' He mocked the appetite the mountain air had given her the last weeks, having eaten as much as any man.

'It isn't that,' she choked, seeming to have trouble stopping the tears now that they had started.

'Then what is it?' His voice hardened. 'Are you

afraid you won't be able to survive here without the—companionship, my cousin has been providing?'

The insult was completely unwarranted, and her tears dried immediately. 'For your information, Mr Whitney,' she said icily, pushing him away from her, 'I have slept alone every night since my arrival here.'

'Why?'

'W—why?' she echoed in a puzzled voice. 'I don't know what you mean.'

He shrugged. 'Kenny would have been more than willing to share your bed. And I'm sure that some of my men wouldn't be averse to it either,' he added mockingly.

She flushed her indignation, her near hysteria of a few moments ago all but forgotten. 'You keep referring to them as "your" men in that arrogant way,' she snapped to hide how deeply he had wounded her with his assumption. She had heard all the old clichés about young widows since her husband had died, the most popular crudely being 'once you've had it you can't do without it', but she had only ever had one lover in her life, and that had been Gavin. She hadn't been in any hurry to replace him on the intimate side of her life, and not being a very sensual person herself she hadn't found that too difficult. Unlike some people, she didn't believe life, and happiness, revolved around the physical.

Kyle raised dark brows at her criticism. 'Shouldn't I?'

The argument was ridiculous, she could see that. They were stuck here, possibly for several days—she refused to think it could be any longer than that!—and to argue about such a trivial matter when their lives could ultimately be in jeopardy was fruitless.'This is stupid.' She stood up with impatient movements, the blanket securely in place. 'We're alone out here, and somehow we have to survive, any unpleasantness between us is pointless.'

For a moment he seemed to hesitate, then he too stood up. 'I'll put something on your forehead.'

'It doesn't really hurt——'

'No senseless arguments, remember?' he mocked, as he opened the full medicine cabinet kept in the kitchen area.

She stood perfectly still while he administered to the cuts on her forehead, doing her best not to look up at him, although it wasn't easy in the circumstances. A faint aroma of male aftershave clung to his skin, and with this came the realisation that he already had more than just a five o'clock shadow. Obviously he was one of those men who needed to shave twice a day.

'You'll have to grow a beard,' she said inconsequentially, blushing as he looked down at her with taunting grey eyes. And for someone who rarely blushed she was doing it a lot lately. Somehow this man had the power to make her feel incredibly young, gauche almost. It wasn't a pleasant sensation.

'I guess I can stand that if you can,' he drawled.

'What do you mean?' she frowned.

He finished putting the adhesive tape in place. 'I've been told that a beard doesn't suit me.'

She felt sure that it wasn't so much that it wouldn't suit him; it would just cover too much of that ruggedly handsome face, would make him look almost demonic. 'I can stand it,' she muttered, turning away. 'I'll get our dinner now.'

She was aware of those watchful grey eyes on her as she worked, was unaware of how attractive she looked with her hair soft about her make-upless face, the blanket revealing more of the perfection of her body than she realised—or would have wanted had she known.

Now that they had decided not to argue they seemed to have little to say to each other, the impromptu stew she had made from the tinned meat and dried vegetables eaten in silence.

'You really can cook,' Kyle said appreciatively after downing two platefuls. 'We could do with you out here at branding time, Charlie is the worst cook I know.'

She gave the ghost of a smile at his attempt at light conversation, exhaustion making her slow to react to what she knew was a standard joke at the Double K. Everyone made derogatory remarks about Charlie Peterson's cooking, but Shelby had a feeling it was done more out of affection for the old man than from any real truth. 'Your aunt told me she taught him herself,' she said as she cleared the table of their crockery, putting it in the soapy water she had boiled.

Kyle grimaced. 'That statement should speak for itself.'

Helen Whitney was one of the best cooks she had ever met; now she knew the jokes were only teasing. Kenny's mother ran the ranch-house with an iron will that matched that of her nephew, and Shelby had come to like her very much.

'Let me do this,' Kyle gently moved her away from the sink, his expression searching. 'You look as if you're about all in. Get some sleep now, everything will seem different in the morning.'

She certainly hoped so, because everything

seemed very bleak right now! Maybe tomorrow she would have the strength and mental capacity to ask him exactly what he had meant about Kenny. Right now she just wanted to sleep.

She did exactly that as soon as her head touched the pillow, heavily at first, and then the dreams began to intrude, dark frightening dreams of the snow falling in on her and burying her, bringing her to startled wakefulness. She looked about her dazedly for several minutes, despair washing over her as she realised where she was.

One of the lamps still burnt low in the cabin, and glancing at the man who slept across the room from her Shelby knew it wasn't for Kyle's benefit. He lay on his back, the face that could often be harsh and derisive smoothed out to look incredibly handsome, although the darkness of the beard that was already forming gave him a rugged look. His quilt had fallen back almost to his waist, his deeply tanned chest covered with dark wiry hair. It was a long time since she had seen a man even partially naked, and it was even more disturbing that Kyle Whitney should now be that man.

She turned away abruptly, feeling almost guilty for noticing the hard planes of his body, the skin a deep mahogany colour. She was in love with Kenny, and the attraction of his cynical cousin didn't matter to her!

And yet her gaze was drawn again and again to him, sleep eluding her. It sounded as if it were snowing again outside, and her heart sank at this further obstacle to them getting away from here, a closed-in feeling enveloping her until she began to move about restlessly.

'Can't you sleep?'

She turned sharply at the sound of that soft

rasp, blinking as she saw Kyle Whitney was now turned on his side as he leaned on his elbow looking across at her. She moistened her lips nervously. 'I'm sorry if I woke you,' her own voice came out in a whisper too.

'You didn't,' he dismissed. 'Does your head ache?'

'My head . . .?'

'Where you fell and knocked it earlier,' he explained patiently.

'Oh. No,' she shook her head. 'I—It feels fine.'

'Then why aren't you asleep?'

How could she tell him it was because the sight of his nakedness had disturbed her! God, she must be going insane, or snow-crazy! She disliked Kyle Whitney, and he despised her, so how could she possibly be physically disturbed by him?

'Shelby?'

She shivered as she turned to find narrowed grey eyes on her. 'I—It was the storm outside,' she invented.

'Was it?' He clearly wasn't convinced.

She gave him a startled look. Surely he hadn't been able to guess the intimacy of her thoughts a few minutes ago? 'I don't know what you mean?' she frowned.

Kyle sat up completely, wrapping a blanket around his waist as he moved to throw more logs on the fire, his expression harsh as he stared down into the leaping flames.

'Kyle?' she prompted at his prolonged silence.

The eyes he turned on her were flinty with contempt. 'Are you finding it lonely already?' he rasped.

All colour left her face as he once again verbally attacked her. 'I told you,' she was breathing erratically, 'I'm used to sleeping alone.'

'But you aren't alone, are you,' he pointed out as he crossed the room towards her.

She blinked as his meaning became crystal clear, realising how dangerous he could be in this frame of mind. 'We don't even like each other——'

'Does that matter?' he scorned.

'To *me*, yes!' she answered indignantly.

'Why?' He sat on the edge of her bed, so near Shelby could feel his body warmth. 'I can assure you I'm much more experienced than Kenny is,' he added derisively.

Shelby moistened suddenly dry lips. This was one way in which she had never thought of Kyle Whitney as being a threat, secure in the knowledge that he didn't like her. 'Are you sure you aren't the one who's lonely, Kyle?' she taunted to hide her fear. 'For Mrs Judd?' she added insultingly, the only occasions Kyle had left the ranch during the last two weeks having been on the evenings he visited the other woman.

His face darkened. 'Sylvia happens to be the widow of my closest friend,' he told her coldly. 'I keep a protective eye on her, that's all.'

'I'm sure you do!'

'Chase would have done the same for me,' he ground out.

'In the same way?' she derided. 'Then it must indeed have been a "close" friendship the two of you had!'

She knew she had gone too far even as he reached for her, expecting to be shaken until her teeth rattled, instead finding herself pulled up against his hair-roughened chest, the quilt falling down so that her bared breasts were crushed against him, the nipples over-sensitive where she hadn't been touched so intimately in such a long time.

The colour flooded her cheeks as Kyle leant back to view her instantaneous reaction, his eyes darkening to black pools of desire. 'Kyle, please——'

'You have beautiful breasts,' he murmured as if she hadn't protested, bending his head to suck one of the pert tips into his mouth, his dark lashes fanned out against his cheeks as he became intent on arousing her with the sharp nip of his teeth and the moist caresses of his tongue.

Shelby's hands came up to push him away, but as the quick-fire excitement surged through her body her fingers curled into him in spasmodic pleasure. Always a sensitive part of her body, her nipples ached for the caress of that moist mouth, her breath catching in her throat as Kyle gave the other breast his full attention.

'Like ivory velvet,' he muttered against her skin, trailing a path of warm kisses down to her navel as he lay her back on the bed, his tongue, tasting her, *exciting* her. 'But you're warm,' he said softly as he moved even lower. 'So very warm.' His hand moved slowly from her knee to her thighs, gently parting them. His mouth traced circles on her skin.

It was madness, utter madness to let him continue, and yet this seemed to be a time out of time, almost a dream. And she didn't want to wake up, had never known such a wealth of sensual delight. Gavin had been a very gentle and considerate lover, he would never have dreamt of silencing her reluctance in such a blatantly physical way.

Gavin. God, if not for herself she had to stop this for him, out of respect for his memory, and the warm and loving relationship they had always had. By acting like a wanton she was not only being unfaithful to that memory she was also convincing Kyle that he had been right about her all along, that any man would do to share her bed in an emergency.

But even so it took some seconds for her to formulate enough strength of will to stop him, her body moving and reacting to his slightest command, opening to him as it had never done before, burning with a need to reach fulfilment.

But Shelby couldn't let herself reach that fulfilment, no matter how much she needed or wanted it, her fingers rough in his hair as she pulled him up to her. 'I meant please stop,' she lied, her pride already in shreds. 'Please stop kissing me, Kyle.'

For a moment he looked dazed, then cold reality returned to the bleakness of his eyes, his mouth twisting as he looked down at her flushed nakedness. 'But I didn't kiss you, Shelby,' he pointed out softly. 'Not here, at least,' he touched her lips with a hand that smelt of her body.

Confusion washed over her as she realised he only spoke the truth. He hadn't kissed her mouth, not once had he acknowledged her with that intimacy. She had been a female body for him to arouse and caress, she as a person hadn't mattered to him, he couldn't have shown her that any more clearly.

He looked down at her with coldly merciless eyes. 'Should I apologise for showing you I was right about you?' he derided with contempt.

She swallowed hard. 'No . . .!'

'Don't look so stricken, Shelby,' he moved back to his own bed, his expression mocking as she instantly pulled the quilt up over her nakedness. 'I was merely saving you the trouble of trying your wiles on me now that Kenny has put himself out of the running.'

'I——'

'You see I'm not interested in more than slightly used goods,' he added sneeringly. 'And certainly not a woman on the make like you are.'

Shelby was very pale, from the shock of her own actions as much as from his insults. She was about to marry his cousin, she deserved every insult he hurled at her about her morals! 'You're so wrong about me,' she began pleadingly.

'Am I?' His eyes looked her over coldly, making Shelby conscious of her tousled hair, languorous green eyes, and passion swollen lips. 'Then what would you call what happened between us just now?' he scorned. 'An impulse?'

'I don't know what happened just now!' she blushed, knowing *exactly* what had almost happened. It had been so long for her, so very long, since a man had looked at her the way he had, since she had ached to be touched. But it shouldn't have happened with this man, should never have happened at all. 'It doesn't mean that I want or expect anything from you——'

He gave a harshly humourless laugh. 'What could you possibly *expect* from me?'

'I just told you, nothing——'

'Too damn right I owe you nothing!' he rasped grimly. 'I think I should warn you now that I don't react well to blackmail, no matter how charmingly it's presented.'

Shelby gasped. 'I didn't——'

'It sounded suspiciously like it to me.' He looked at her coldly. 'I made love to you just now for one reason and one reason only, to prove to you that no matter what opinion you may have of what you're doing *I* know that any man will do for you. But I don't intend being Kenny's replacement, not in bed or in a monetary way. I realise this set-back with Kenny must have upset your plans somewhat, but it would take more than a little seduction on your part to make me offer you marriage.'

'I didn't seduce you,' she protested. 'You were the one who came to my bed!'

'After I found your gaze on me like a caress,' he scorned. 'You were begging for me to make love to you.'

'No!'

'Yes,' he hissed. 'But little mercenaries like you don't interest me in more than a fleeting capacity.' His gaze flickered over her contemptuously. 'I hope I make myself clear?'

'You think of me as a one-night stand,' she said disgustedly.

'How aptly put,' he derided with distaste. 'I knew exactly what you were and what you were after before we even met,' he added with disgust.

'And that is?' she prompted stiffly.

'Surely it's obvious?'

'I'd like to hear, nonetheless.'

He shrugged. 'After the life you've lived Kenny must have seemed like a heaven-sent opportunity,' he scorned. 'He was young and alone, and far from home, an easy conquest for the lonely little widow,' his mouth twisted, 'Thank God he came to his senses in time!'

'The life I've lived?' she prompted an explanation, not understanding what he meant. As far as she knew her life had been nothing out of the ordinary. This man obviously didn't agree with her.

'You're very young to have been left a widow to fend for yourself. I'm sure that when you married your husband you envisaged a long and happy life with him, maybe even contemplated having children,' he added as if he doubted it.

'Is that so unusual?' she frowned.

'No,' Kyle shook his head. 'But he had the inconvenience to go and die on you.'

'That's a foul thing to say!' she choked on her anger. 'I loved my husband very much.'

'The same way you love Kenny?' he dismissed. 'That sort of love isn't worth having.'

'And what would you know about any sort of love?' she accused insultingly.

His mouth tightened. 'I know that a year after your husband's death, this man you're supposed to have loved, you were tired of trying to make it alone, of working in a hairdressing salon to support yourself——'

'I don't just work in the salon, I *own* it,' she told him forcefully.

'And I'm sure the profit you make just about covers the cost of your rent and costs!'

'You don't know what you're talking about!'

'I know that you saw Kenny for a fool, a fool who could give you back the life of relative ease you no doubt enjoyed with your husband. But don't take me for the same kind of fool, Shelby, because I can assure you I'm far from being that. Far from it!' he repeated with feeling.

She knew that, what she didn't know was where he could have gained such an impression of her. Oh he had all the basic facts right, he just had the conclusions all wrong. And she didn't understand why. 'Where did you get your information from?' she asked slowly.

'Some of it from Kenny,' he shrugged. 'The rest I pieced together myself.'

She wondered which parts were which, but

was reluctant to ask him in the circumstances. 'Then we both know where we stand, don't we?' she said softly.

'Yes!' he grated.

'Then we may as well go back to sleep,' she yawned as if to add to her impression of tiredness, whereas in reality she had too much on her mind to fall asleep. 'And hope we can get out of here tomorrow,' she added hopefully, needing desperately to talk to Kenny, knowing that only he could supply the answers she needed.

'I wouldn't count on it,' Kyle muttered roughly.

'Oh but I am,' she said with heartfelt feeling as she turned on her side towards the wall, remaining that way, determined not to even look at him to see if he had fallen back to sleep.

Her thoughts were racing, dark unhappy thoughts as she remembered the conversation she had had with Kenny yesterday, a conversation that on reflection seemed to have turned her life about once again. She had thought Kenny understood at the time, that it hadn't mattered to him, but now she wasn't so sure. The facts that his family seemed to have about her, facts only he could have told them, seemed to conflict with reality, making her wonder why he had lied to them.

Worst of all, she was no longer sure her wandering off in the blizzard had been an accident!

CHAPTER THREE

SHE hadn't deliberately set out to deceive anyone, had always intended Kenny to know the truth about her, she just hadn't thought it important enough to mention to him before now. Everything had happened so fast since her arrival in Montana, Kenny's proposal only two days later, and then the frantic wedding preparations, that they had barely had a moment to themselves to talk about anything, let alone something so private.

But yesterday they had stolen a couple of hours to themselves, and Shelby had chosen that time to tell Kenny about Gavin and her marriage to him. He had listened without a flicker of emotion to all that she had to say, had seemed to treat her the same as he usually did for the rest of the day.

But he had gone to see Wendy when he had known she was lost, possibly in danger, which didn't speak of a man in love. She didn't even consider the fact that Kyle could have lied to her about that, Kyle Whitney was basically a truthful man, he wouldn't lie to achieve his objective of getting her out of Kenny's life. She seemed to have done that effectively herself! How could she have even guessed that Kenny would react the way that he seemed to have done to what she had told him? Not that it hadn't been important, she knew that it was, but she hadn't thought it would matter to a man like Kenny. Obviously it did.

Her love for him refused to die completely, wouldn't do that until she had heard the truth

46

from him herself. But it was her pride that hurt her the most right now. She had been reluctant to become involved with Kenny in the first place, had been persuaded into going out with him by his boyish charm. It hurt to now think that boyish charm had all been a pose, that she hadn't been his main interest at all. Because she knew now exactly what had been.

Did Kyle realise what sort of man his cousin was? Somehow she doubted it, the two men seeming the best of friends. And if she could be fooled by Kenny, after having been suspicious of all entanglements since Gavin's death, then what chance did Kyle have?

God, she felt so humiliated! She had placed her whole life and happiness in Kenny's hands and he had thrown them back at her as if she meant nothing to her. What sort of man was he, how could he——

'Still can't sleep?'

She stiffened as Kyle asked her that question for a second time tonight, but she made no reply, feigning sleep, letting the tears fall silently for the pain and humiliation she had suffered at Kenny's selfish hands.

'Shelby?' Kyle prompted in a whisper, not convinced by her act at all.

Again she ignored him, not wanting to speak to him now, needing the protection of silence against his rapier tongue, knowing that with his suspicious mind he was sure to misunderstand the reason for her tears. He had ridiculed her enough for one night, and he obviously didn't know the full truth about her, the real reason Kenny had changed his mind about marrying her, and until she had spoken to Kenny she didn't care to discuss it with him.

She lay in frozen in silence as she waited for his next action, hearing a rustle of movement, tensing even more as she waited for his touch. But long seconds later she knew that he had only turned over to go to sleep, the deeply even tenor of his breathing seconds later letting her know that he had done exactly that.

But sleep still eluded her, the pain of Kenny's betrayal slowly breaking her heart. She had been willing to give up everything for him, but it seemed that some sacrifices weren't enough—and some just too much!

She was alone in the cabin when she woke the next morning, the bunk across from her already neatly made, the smell of brewed coffee filling the snug interior of the room.

It took her a few minutes of alienation to become aware of her surroundings, to realise she was indeed marooned in a mountain cabin with Kyle Whitney. Somehow during the night it had all come to seem like a particularly bad nightmare.

But as she looked about her she knew it was true, the real rusticity of the cabin becoming apparent in the light of day, looking exactly what it was, a summer stopover for several of the ruggedly self-sufficient men Kyle and Kenny employed, the furniture and cooking utensils primitive to say the least.

But the wind had stopped howling outside, so hopefully the snow had stopped falling too, the cabin now shrouded in an eerie silence. Surely Kyle wouldn't have gone off and left her here without waking her first? She knew he was a man capable of anything!

She hastily got out of bed, shivering in spite of the warmly glowing fire, looking around for her clothes. Her denims and jumper were lying at the foot of her bed, a further search locating her bra and panties lying across a chair, put there to dry in front of the fire after being washed. And Shelby knew she hadn't been the one to wash them! There was something very unsettling about thinking of Kyle Whitney touching the delicate lace wisps that were her underclothes. No one else could have been responsible for them being freshly laundered. He must have done it after she fell asleep for the first time.

Her wash after she had dressed was little more than a splashing on of water, putting on her thick outer clothing so that she could go in search of Kyle. He may not be her idea of the perfect companion but for the moment he was all she had got!

The scene that met her eyes as she stepped out into the crisp air made her stop in wonder. Everywhere she looked she could see snow, a clean pristine blanket of it over everything, the closely packed pine trees, the cabin, the distant mountains. It was all so beautiful it took her breath away, totally eliminating any feelings of danger she might have had last night. It was all like a scene from a Christmas card, the sort she had always liked to receive.

'So Her Majesty has deigned to get up, hmm?' Kyle Whitney's harshly derisive voice cut into the beauty of the day. 'How nice!' he added with extra sarcasm.

Shelby flushed at the jibe, turning to find him beside the wood pile he had pulled a tarpaulin back to reveal, his footprints around the cabin the only break in the pure white snow. He was obviously in the middle of bringing in more logs for the fire, and there was no knowing how long he had been up and about. Some time, from his sarcasm!

'You could have woken "Her Majesty",' she said sharply. 'I just overslept, that's all.' And she knew the reason for that. It had been well into the early hours of the morning before she fell asleep for a second time, although as far as she knew Kyle had been asleep long before that.

'How unusual,' he said dryly.

She frowned. 'What do you mean?'

He shrugged, piling more logs into his arms, his muscles tautening beneath his coat. 'From what I hear Mrs O'Neal likes to stay in bed until all hours of the morning.'

She flushed at the rebuke. 'If you're talking about since I arrived here——'

'Well of course I am, Shelby,' he taunted mockingly, eyeing her speculatively. 'How would I know of your sleeping habits when you're in London! I can assure you Kenny isn't the sort to "kiss and tell".'

'Because there's nothing to tell!' She wasn't a person easily driven to anger, but at that moment she could quite cheerfully have stamped her foot in frustration—if it wouldn't have looked so ridiculous in feet of snow. 'I thought we agreed last night that we wouldn't argue any more?'

'That was the first time you went to sleep,' his eyes had iced over. 'Later it was a different matter,' he added harshly. 'That changed things.'

She avoided his gaze, her memories of last night as vivid as his obviously were. 'I'm sorry you feel that way,' she mumbled. 'I'm also sorry I didn't wake up earlier this morning. As for when I first arrived at the ranch, there is such a thing as jet-lag, you know.'

'I know,' he nodded, moving past her with the logs. 'I've flown a few times myself,' he taunted.

Shelby knew that he flew the Whitney plane. 'I'm sorry if you feel I was a little tardy when I first arrived,' she said stiffly. 'But my nights were suddenly days, and vice versa. And besides, I only slept late a couple of mornings, the rest of the time I've been up helping your aunt at seven o'clock,' she defended.

'Well if you haven't been sleeping with Kenny I suppose you had to earn your keep somehow!' He disappeared inside the cabin with the logs.

Shelby was left speechless. This man never let up, did he, insult after insult flowed easily from his lips. And they hurt. She had never been subjected to such blistering dislike from a man in all of her twenty-five years. Gavin had always been kind, before and during their marriage, and Kenny had always been a gentleman around her too. Maybe she had been spoilt by the two most important men in her life, but never before had she been the recipient of the blatant dislike Kyle Whitney subjected her to.

He gave her only a cursory glance as he came out to get more logs. 'If you have nothing better to do than stand around looking beautiful perhaps you wouldn't mind getting us some breakfast?' His lightly veiled sarcasm didn't hide the fact that he was once again insulting her, even the fact that he recognised she was beautiful not taking the edge off his words.

She watched as he picked up several of the logs at a time, knowing from experience how heavy they could be individually, and yet he seemed to have no trouble managing half-a-dozen or more at a time. 'I'll help you with that first, if you like,' she offered, determined to be friendly.

He gave her a scathing look. 'Stick to what you know, Shelby,' he dismissed.

Her mouth twisted at his derision. 'Meaning a woman's place is in the kitchen?'

He eyed her speculatively. 'Not necessarily,' he drawled after a long, pointed silence.

Shelby flushed at his intended innuendo. 'How long do you intend to keep this up?' she snapped.

He shrugged past her with more logs, and this time Shelby followed him inside, her eyes widening as she saw just how much firewood he had brought in; it looked as if they were in for a siege!

She turned slowly to look at him. 'Just how long do you think we're going to be here?'

He straightened, flexing his straining muscles. 'It never hurts to be prepared,' he dismissed her concern.

Shelby met his gaze steadily. 'How long?' she prompted again with stubbornness.

He shrugged. 'It could be any time——'

'For God's sake, Kyle,' she snapped. 'I'm not a child, so don't treat me like one!'

His mouth thinned, and she knew he wasn't used to being spoken to in this way, by anyone. 'I don't see the point in both of us worrying——'

'Then you are worried?' she pounced.

'I'm—concerned,' he amended slowly. 'We aren't really that far in miles from the ranch, but in this weather we might as well be a few hundred. You asked for the truth,' he rasped as she went pale.

'Please go on,' she invited stiffly.

'There isn't a lot more to say,' he sighed.

'We're about twenty miles from the ranch, across some of the roughest terrain on the Double K. Until the weather breaks we'll just have to sit tight.'

Her spirits sank even lower. 'You don't think anyone will be out looking for us?'

'If you're thinking of Kenny, then forget it,' he said grimly. 'And anyone else who might want to come looking will be hampered by the weather.'

'But won't they be worried about you?' she frowned.

'Probably,' he dismissed with a casualness she knew he must be far from feeling.

'I'm sorry, Kyle. I really am.' She looked at him imploringly.

Devilment darkened his eyes. 'Sorry enough to cook my breakfast?' he mocked.

She smiled her relief at his first ever show of teasing around her. 'Yes,' she still smiled. 'Although I could help you with the logs first.'

He shook his head. 'There's no need, I'm almost through. Besides,' he drawled, 'you may not have noticed last night but there isn't a whole lot to do here.'

'Sorry?' She frowned her ignorance.

'As you've already pointed out,' he said dryly, 'we could be here several days, and although this may be an insult to your feminine pride, boredom could become a problem.'

Her smile faded as his humour was predictably followed by a caustic comment. But at least he wasn't treating her like an idiot now, someone he could humour about the real danger they were in. 'I saw some books in the cabin——'

'Do you like Westerns?' Kyle derided.

'Less and less,' she replied pointedly.

He chuckled softly, lines grooved beside his

mouth. 'It isn't quite as they portray it in the movies, is it?'

'Not quite,' she agreed dryly. 'Although I didn't do too badly on my hero.' She knew she had said the wrong thing again as suspicion darkened his eyes. 'Just think, it could have been Charlie who found me,' she tried to lighten his mood again, knowing she had only partially succeeded when his eyes remained flinty.

'You would probably have got more sympathy from Charlie,' he told her softly.

She didn't doubt it for a minute, the elderly man very much like a father-figure. But she doubted he would have been able to instil the confidence in her that Kyle did. They may dislike each other intensely but she didn't doubt for one moment Kyle's ability to get them both out of this. 'I'll settle for the hero I've got,' she said huskily.

Kyle looked less than pleased by this remark too. 'And I'll settle for my breakfast,' he rasped.

It was meant to be a verbal slap in the face, and it had the same effect as a physical one would have done. 'Coming up,' she muttered.

The pancakes she prepared did little to sweeten Kyle's mood, and he excused himself from the cabin as soon as he had finished eating. Unsure of exactly where he was going—he certainly didn't tell her—Shelby was left to her own devices for the morning. Meticulously clean and tidy in her own home she decided the cabin wouldn't hurt for being cleaned up a little.

She swept the floor, tidied the beds, dusted and cleaned every surface she could find. And for all the notice Kyle took of her efforts when he came back for his lunch she might as well have saved herself the trouble. He ate down the food she had prepared without saying a word.

'I'm beginning to feel like one of America's pioneer women,' she finally remarked lightly, only picking at her own food, stew as a staple diet for the next few days not something she relished.

Kyle looked up uninterestedly. 'Hm?'

She looked at him with widely innocent eyes. 'Well I believe it was quite normal then for the men not to talk to their women unless it was absolutely necessary to.'

His mouth tightened at the taunt. 'You aren't my woman. And I have nothing to say. This isn't London, Shelby, where people sit around all day making idle conversation in idle lives.'

She sighed, clearing away the plates to replace them with the tinned fruit they had for dessert. 'You could tell me what you did with your morning,' she prompted without rancour, knowing that his accusation about some people's idle conversation was true in some cases, although not in her own. She didn't have the time.

He shrugged. 'I took a look around the immediate area.'

She looked at him sharply. 'Why? You seem to know the cabin pretty well, I thought you would be familiar with its surroundings too.'

'I am,' he drawled. 'I'm also familiar with the fact that a storm like the one we had yesterday can change the landscape within hours. It can also make surrounding trees unsafe. Hell, the cold alone is enough to do that.'

She swallowed hard. 'And are there any, unsafe ones, I mean?'

'Not so far, no.'

'So far?' She watched him as he stood up to pull on his thick coat and gloves. 'You aren't going out again?' She couldn't hide her disappointment.

He gave her a look that clearly told her he disliked over-curious, clinging women. 'It will be dark early,' he nodded. 'And we could be in for another storm later.'

'Oh but——'

'I shouldn't be long,' he cut in firmly. 'And keep the fire going,' he instructed curtly before leaving.

Shelby glared after him with dislike. She wasn't stupid, had kept the fire going all morning in his absence, knew they had to keep it going, and not just because there was a shortage of matches. It had taken most of the previous night to get the cabin as warm as it was, and she was well aware of the fact that Kyle had been up several times in the night putting logs on the fire to keep it that way.

She felt more and more like one of those downtrodden women of the first American settlers as she cleared away the debris from their lunch, a spark of rebellion urging her to get out of the cabin once she had cleaned away, needing to get out into the air for a while.

The cold was very deceptive, and for the first few minutes of her walk she didn't even realise how cold it was, the air crisp and fresh, not damp as it would have been in England in the same weather.

She walked to keep the chill from her bones, always keeping the smoking chimney of the cabin in sight as she did so. Kyle would allow her no mercy if he had to come looking for her again! Not that he had given her much the first time.

But despite what he had said about checking the immediate area of the cabin she didn't find him, only the odd set of footprints that seemed to lead back into themselves. She had intended to join him, as he hadn't proffered the invitation himself, but as she couldn't even find him that was impossible. She wandered back to the cabin with despondent movements, going inside to warm herself, looking uninterestedly through the books on the shelf, finding them all to be Westerns as Kyle had warned they would be. Having had her fill of the 'modern cowboy' for the moment, she was loath to read about the even more ruthless exploits of the olden day ones.

Bored and listless she pulled on her anorak again, angry with Kyle for just leaving her to her own devices for the entire day. He could have spent *some* time with her, damn him!

The smooth beauty of the snow beyond the cabin beckoned her on her second walk out, crying out for the ice-cold beauty to be disturbed by human presence. Where the spark of mischief came from that urged her to build the snowman she didn't know. She hadn't made one since she was a very young child, and yet suddenly it was what she most wanted to do.

Once started she threw herself into the task with gusto, the snowman almost as tall as herself as she searched around for something to put on the top as the eyes, nose, and mouth of the face. In the end she went back to the cabin for splinters of wood, and was just putting the finishing touches to the mouth when she sensed she was no longer alone.

The hysterical images of bears and wolves that had so terrified her the previous day no longer even occurred to her, and she knew instantly who was behind her.

'True English spirit,' Kyle drawled derisively.

'We're stranded out here and you're building a snowman!'

She bent slowly to pick up a handful of snow, crushing it into the semblance of a ball shape as she turned to face him. 'And snowballs,' she warned as the snow left her glove-covered hand in aim for his face.

It was a direct hit, much to her delight, the surprised expression on Kyle's face as the melting snow slowly trickled down his face making her laugh as much as her satisfaction did.

'Why you little——!' Retaliation gleamed in his eyes as he bent to pick up some snow, his aim even better than hers had been as he caught her directly on the nose.

As with building the snowman it was years since she had thrown snowballs, her laugh light with happiness as they began to throw snow at each other in earnest.

Kyle's aim was so much better than hers, that within minutes she was liberally sprayed with snow, her hat having fallen off during the exchange, her loosened hair gleaming brightly, it a little wet too now.

'Enough!' she gasped as yet another handful of snow caught her directly in the face, smiling as she walked over to him, her eyes gleaming with happiness as she fell against him. 'You win,' she was breathing heavily from the exertion.

Kyle looked down at her with admiring eyes, his hood pushed back to reveal his dark hair, his arm going about her shoulders in companionable enjoyment. 'We'll call it a draw,' he told her softly. 'After all, you struck the first blow.'

'Yes,' she was still breathing heavily, falling weakly to sit down in the snow. 'I think I must be out of condition,' she looked up at him beneath lowered lashes, mischief in the stormy green depths of her eyes.

'Here,' he held out his hand to her.

That was exactly what Shelby had been hoping he would do, the gleam of devilment deepening in her eyes as she took the proffered hand, and instead of allowing him to pull her to her feet pulled him off balance.

'Shelby . . .!' he had time to cry his surprise before he landed face-down in the snow at her side.

With an agility that hadn't been present in her movements a few seconds earlier she jumped to her feet, laughing gleefully as Kyle turned over to spit the snow from his mouth. 'Now I've struck the first *and* last blow,' she said with satisfaction, grinning at how funny he looked covered in snow, even the darkness of his hair sprinkled with it. 'How the mighty are fallen,' she taunted with relish.

He became suddenly still, his eyes narrowed, his mouth suddenly curving into a smile that was as dangerous as he was. 'This fight is far from over,' he warned softly.

Shelby felt the thrill of apprehension run through her, her eyes darkening in anticipation. 'Don't you like being defeated by a mere woman?' she challenged.

He looked up at her calmly. 'I'm not beaten yet.'

'You look it to me,' she raised auburn brows.

'Looks can sometimes be deceiving,' he drawled.

Even though he was still sitting firmly on the ground he seemed threatening, and the urge to show him that he didn't frighten her in the least had her bending down to gather up more snow, putting it down the back of his neck and running off before he could catch her.

'You're one very provoking woman!' he growled as he stood up, his movements unhurried as he followed her through the snow, gaining on her all the time.

'It was only a game, Kyle,' she pleaded as she looked out at him from behind the protection of a pine tree.

His eyes were dark with satisfaction. 'I know that,' he nodded. But still he came towards her, a look of determination to his strong mouth.

She moved to another tree further away. 'Then why do I get the distinct impression that you've stopped playing,' she asked nervously.

His teeth gleamed whitely against his darkly tanned skin. 'I'm still playing, Shelby, it's just that I've changed the rules a little.'

She swallowed hard. 'It was only a little harmless fun,' she protested at the retribution he promised.

'So will tanning your hide be!'

'Kyle . . .?'

His grin deepened at her nervousness, and although he was nothing like the grim-faced man she had come to expect he was still very dangerous.

'Kyle, I was only joking,' she told him desperately as she began to run once again.

'I'm not,' he followed at a much more leisurely pace, his long strides gaining on her all the time.

'No one has ever hit me,' she gasped her alarm at the prospect as she realised the walk in the heavy snow and building the snowman had indeed taken their toll on her, her legs feeling heavier by the second.

'Then it's about time someone did!' He made a

lunge for her, catching her about the waist, the snow absorbing their fall, Shelby's struggles to be free ineffectual against Kyle's superior strength and weight.

Finally she lay still, her arms held captive above her head, her breasts rising and falling as she breathed her exhaustion. 'Would it do any good if I were to say I'm sorry?' she asked hopefully.

'It might,' he nodded.

'Then I am.'

Kyle shook his head. 'It doesn't help the fact that I have icy cold snow dripping down my back.'

Her eyes widened with indignation. 'But you said that if I apologised——'

'That it might do some good,' he acknowledged softly, easily turning her over so that she lay across his knees. 'It didn't,' he laughed as his hand came down painfully on her denim-clad bottom. 'But this will.'

Shelby's screams of outrage carried far and clear in the stillness of the day, but they had little real effect, Kyle not stopping the punishment until he was satisfied she had been suitably subdued.

She glared at him as he turned her over. 'Are you satisfied now?' she snapped.

His mouth quirked with humour at her indignation. 'It didn't really hurt.'

'Tell that to my bottom!' She angrily rubbed the pained part of her anatomy.

'I'd love to,' he drawled suggestively.

Colour darkened her cheeks. 'Kyle——'

'Dear God, but you're beautiful,' he groaned as his head swooped and his mouth claimed hers.

She was initially too surprised to object, and

then as his lips infused warm life into her body she didn't want to, her arms going up about his neck as he cradled her against his chest, both of them forgetting their surroundings, the coldness of the snow they were sitting in, the fact that seconds ago they had been arguing as usual.

They certainly weren't arguing now, one of Kyle's hands capturing her chin so that he wasn't thwarted in his languorous plundering of her mouth, his lips moving across and into hers with slow eroticism, preparing her for the intimacy of his tongue probing between her teeth to the warm softness beneath, searching out every sensitive nuance of her mouth even as his thighs throbbing against her cried out for an even deeper possession.

Shelby's hair splayed out bright red as Kyle lay her back in the snow, her hat lying on the ground near the snowman, her body arching up into his as he moved to lie across her, her eyes dark with longing, the last hour seeming to wipe out all the unpleasantness between them.

'We pick the damndest places for this,' Kyle muttered before his mouth claimed hers again, fiercer this time, drawing her into him, blocking out all thought but the two of them in this ritual of lovemaking.

Shelby's hands were tangled in his hair as she willingly allowed him to lead her into the sensual abyss that had so long been denied her, his bitter rejection of her the previous evening not seeming to matter as he shuddered against her with a desire he couldn't hide.

In the circumstances it was a miracle that Shelby heard the overhead sound of the engine, lost as she was in a world where only the magic of Kyle's mouth and hands seemed to matter, her hips crushed against his much more powerful ones as he cupped her bottom into him.

But somehow she did hear the engine, only slightly at first, so distant she imagined she actually had a buzzing in her ears from the onslaught of passion that had engulfed them. But the noise became louder and louder, filling her head now, until her lids widened up at the sky to see a small red-and-white bird above them in the sky. Only it wasn't a bird, it was a plane!

'Kyle!' She pushed him away from her excitedly, all the time her gaze fixed on the small plane flying over them, too far away to make out their prone figures in the snow, surely?

Kyle was slower to react to outside stimulus, trying to pull her back into his arms, flames still flickering deeply in the depths of his grey eyes.

'Kyle, it's a plane!' She couldn't take her eyes off it as it began to circle lower, scrambling to her feet. 'It *is* a plane—isn't it?' she voiced uncertainly as Kyle made no effort to get up out of the snow.

He glanced up as the red-and-white bird dipped down above them. 'Yes, it's a plane——'

'God, it is, *it is*!' Shelby's face was alight with excitement as she began to stumble through the snow, waving her arms about frantically in an effort to attract the attention of the pilot.

She knew that the people above may not even be looking for them, may be on a private flight, but if she could just make them see her perhaps they would realise the urgency of the situation down on the ground and report it to someone. She and Kyle were sure to be rescued then, and when they were——

'Oh!' She gave a pained gasp as she tripped over something in her path, her attention having all been up at the sky, falling heavily to the ground as her ankle twisted painfully beneath her. And to add to her misery the plane seemed to have resumed its course and was now disappearing into the grey sky over the mountains.

She could have cried at the futility she felt at that moment, falling back into the cold snow, tears glistening in the dark green despair of her eyes. For a few brief moments she had teetered on the brink of being rescued from this wilderness, and to have it taken from her again so cruelly seemed almost inhuman.

And from the way Kyle was casually strolling over to her, brushing the snow from his clothes, he didn't appear to be in the least perturbed that the one chance they had had of rescue the last two days had just literally flown off into the sunset!

CHAPTER FOUR

THE undignified end to her plea for attention from the occupants of the plane, and now Kyle's near complacency on top of that, filled her with anger. 'Why didn't you try and do something to attract their attention?' she snapped.

Kyle looked down at her with amused eyes. 'Is that what you were trying to do?'

Their rapport as they played in the snow was forgotten as she glared at him, the passion of their kisses a few minutes ago banished to the far recesses of her mind. 'You know damn well I was!'

He shrugged. 'The pilot would never have seen you, no matter how much you waved your arms about.'

She flushed at the taunt. 'You could have tried, damn you,' she cursed herself inwardly as her voice broke emotionally, not wanting him to know how weak and utterly defeated she suddenly felt.

'I told you, there was no point,' he dismissed.

His ability to remain so calmly unmoved after such a moment of hope—no matter how remote!—made her want to scream. 'You might at least offer to help me up,' she rasped.

His mouth quirked. 'The last time I did that *I* landed up in the snow.'

'This is hardly the same situation!'

'No?'

'No!' She struggled to get to her feet on her own, her face paling as she did so, beads of perspiration dampening her brow. But not for anything would she cry out at the pain in her ankle. She moistened her lips, biting down into the softness of her lower one, knowing that she was soon going to have to earn the scorn of the autocratic man who towered over her, because she simply couldn't get up on her own.

Kyle seemed to sense some of her discomfort at that moment, frowning heavily. 'What is it?'

'I—Oh!' she gasped as she moved too quickly and the pain in her ankle became excruciating. 'It's my ankle,' she admitted as Kyle bent down on his haunches beside her. 'I—I think it could be broken.'

He couldn't hide the look of irritation that crossed his face, and he didn't even try to, impatience etched into his face as he swung her up in his arms, turning abruptly in the direction of the cabin, seeming too angry to even speak.

'I couldn't help it,' Shelby finally felt compelled to mutter, her arms up about his neck as he carried her, uncomplaining of the pain the latter caused to her ankle.

Kyle's jaw was rigid as he walked on. 'It seems you never can,' he bit out.

She flushed at the derisive rebuke. 'I was only trying to get us help!'

'And instead you've brought us even more trouble,' he rasped grimly as he deposited her on her bed without preamble, going towards the kitchen area to come back with a knife. 'It's to cut off your boot,' came his exasperated explanation as her eyes widened fearfully.

She could have cried at her foolishness. Of course it was to cut off her boot, what else had she thought it was for! She may be a pain in the neck as far as Kyle was concerned but she didn't think even he would resort to cutting it. 'Isn't cutting my boot off a little drastic?' she pleaded as he moved threateningly towards the fitted leather.

'Can you get it off without it?'

In truth her ankle did feel swollen, and the already fashionably fitted boot was difficult enough to get on and off without that. But she gritted her teeth and pulled at it, determined Kyle shouldn't cut it from her foot and so render her shoeless. The last thing she wanted was to be confined to the cabin indefinitely, although the pain and swelling in her ankle seemed to imply she wouldn't be going very far for a while.

Kyle came down on his haunches beside her to peel off the sock and look at the swollen flesh, hurting her despite the gentleness of his hands. 'I don't think anything is broken,' he said grimly as he tightly bandaged the injured area. 'But you'll have to stay off it until we get back to the ranch and it can be X-rayed.'

Shelby was very pale from the effort it had taken not to cry out as he manipulated her ankle, and as a result she felt irritable and moody. 'And when do you think that will be?' she asked in a disgruntled voice. 'Now that the only chance of rescue we've had has disappeared over the horizon!' she added accusingly.

Kyle straightened, shrugging out of his thick outer clothing. 'If the weather holds off—and by that I mean we don't get any more snow,' he drawled, 'I think we should be picked up some time tomorrow.'

'That's all right for you to say, but— Did you say tomorrow?' she gasped in realisation.

He nodded. 'All being well.'

'But—I—You—How can you be so certain?' she demanded disbelievingly.

'I can't be certain,' he dismissed, filling the kettle and putting it on the boil. 'No one ever can in this climate. The blizzard might start up again tonight and delay things for a few days. But at least they know where we are now, so——'

'They do?' Shelby frowned.

He gave her an impatient look. 'You surely don't think I spent the entire day just looking around?' he derided.

'Well I— You said——' She gave up trying to argue with him, knowing that out here he had all the advantages. God, what she wouldn't give to have him in London for a few weeks, on her own territory, and see how he coped out of his depth in London society. Just the thought of it cheered her up, although she knew it would never happen. According to Kenny most of his cousin's travelling was done within America. 'How did you spend the day?' she asked resignedly.

'Building a marker out on the lake for the plane to see.'

'What lake?' she looked even more puzzled.

'The one just out there.'

Shelby tried to recall a mental picture of the terrain in the direction he pointed, the wide expense of flat white snow at the back of the cabin now taking on more meaning. 'That's a lake?' she realised.

'In the summer it is,' Kyle answered with amusement, handing her the mug of hot coffee. 'In the winter it should make a good helicopter pad.'

She swallowed hard. 'Is it strong enough?' She had a horrifying vision of their rescuers being sucked down to the bottom of the lake as the ice cracked beneath them.

'The ice is feet thick. It will hold,' he nodded confidently.

'Then why couldn't you have told me that earlier?' she snapped her anger.

'Maybe I should have done,' he scowled. 'Then you wouldn't have tried to play the heroine and ended up immobile!'

She flushed at his scorn. 'You can't be sure they saw your marker,' she flashed.

'They saw it,' he nodded. 'They dipped the wings of the plane in acknowledgement.'

No wonder he had looked so unconcerned when the plane flew off, while she had felt all the despair of a near-rescue without a word of comfort from him. Kyle Whitney was not only the most insensitive man she had ever known, he was also the cruellest. But she didn't intend giving him the satisfaction of breaking down in front of him again. 'Then let's hope that the snow holds off for one more day at least,' she said waspishly. 'I can't wait to get away from here!' And you, her tone implied.

He raised dark brows at her vehemence. 'You didn't feel that way a few minutes ago.'

She met his gaze coolly, not pretending to misunderstand him. 'At that time I had no idea how long we were going to be stranded here.'

His mouth tightened. 'And you didn't see any point in antagonising the only other person around when I so obviously wanted to kiss you.'

'Exactly!'

He turned away abruptly. 'I'll get dinner.'

Shelby couldn't tell whether she had angered him or just annoyed him, but she felt elated that she had managed to elicit some reaction. He too often managed to make her feel foolish and inadequate, it felt good to turn the tables on him for once, even if only temporarily.

But her brief moment of elation couldn't make up for the fact that Kyle spoke little throughout the remainder of the evening, picking out one of the paperbacks after dinner and becoming immersed in what was a typical Western tale of shootouts and betrayal, judging by the lurid cover depicting a gun-fight in the middle of a sleepy town's street.

She did her own washing this evening, hopping over to the sink once she had changed into the unbecoming blanket, giving Kyle a grateful smile as he wordlessly pushed a chair in behind her.

'Er—I'll do your things too—if you like,' she offered a few minutes later.

'No, thanks,' he drawled.

'It's no trouble,' she assured him awkwardly.

'I didn't think it would be,' he dismissed. 'But you've been on that ankle long enough for one night, it's time you laid down and rested it.'

She was, in fact, feeling quite tired, but having Kyle more or less order her to bed rankled. She had never let a man make her decisions for her, not even Gavin, and she certainly wasn't about to let the forceful Kyle Whitney be the first to do so. 'I think I'll have another cup of coffee first,' she told him stubbornly. 'Would you like some?'

He eyed her reprovingly over the top of his book, seeming to know the coffee was only a bid for independence and not really something she wanted or needed. 'No, thanks. But you go ahead,' he added uninterestedly.

Shelby flushed her resentment. By giving his permission in that way he had taken all the independence out of the action. 'I don't think I'll

bother,' she muttered, hobbling back to her bed.
'Good night, Kyle,' she called softly once she was
warmly beneath the quilt.

''Night,' he replied abruptly. 'Can I go on
reading for a while or will the light disturb you?'

'No. I mean—please continue to read,' she
invited. 'The light doesn't bother me.'

But the man sitting in the lamp-light did! What
was it about the night hours that made her view
him in this dangerous way? Anyone would think
she really was a love-starved widow who needed a
man to fulfil her. Which was ridiculous. She had
never been that interested in the physical side of a
relationship, and although her nights with Gavin
had been enjoyable they certainly hadn't left her
aching for a man in her bed since his death.

There was something about Kyle that induced
this longing within her, a yearning for the
burning kisses of this afternoon, and with a self-
disgusted groan she turned away from him
towards the wall. She wasn't a very sensually
aware woman, no matter what he might believe to
the contrary, and whatever it was she felt for him
she would fight it at all costs. How scornful he
would feel if he realised her need of him!

He was still reading when she finally fell into a
restless sleep, her dreams consisting of erotic
fantasies, all of them involving Kyle. They
became so real, so very real, that she finally woke
up in a cold sweat, her breathing unsteady as she
turned to look at the man who tormented her. He
seemed deeply asleep, the dark hair ruffled, the
quilt covering his shoulders tonight, the cabin
more chill than it had previously been.

And the reason for that soon became patently
obvious; the fire had burnt down to a few
glowing ashes. Shelby felt a sudden warmth for

the man across the room from her at that
moment, knowing that he had been too tired
tonight to maintain the fire as he had been doing.
It somehow made him seem more human, and
with an understanding smile in his direction she
moved awkwardly across the room to quietly
build up the fire, the flames leaping high among
the logs within a few minutes.

'Shelby?'

She turned so suddenly at the sound of his
voice that she twisted her injured ankle beneath
her and went down on the ground with a pained
cry.

'What the——!' Kyle came fully awake as he
realised her predicament, bounding out of bed to
come towards her.

Even in her discomfort Shelby was aware of his
masculinity, struggling to get to her feet alone,
knowing that in her already vulnerable emotional
state that she couldn't bear it right now if he
touched her. In her efforts to stand up she
dislodged the quilt she had temporarily wrapped
around herself, feeling it fall to the floor at her
feet even as she straightened.

Kyle suddenly stood very still, his body leaping
in response to her golden nakedness, her breasts
pert and upstanding, the nipples deeply brown,
her waist slender, her hips narrow and provocative. He drew in a ragged breath. 'This time I'm
not going to be able to say no,' he warned softly.

She didn't want him to, sinking down on to the
quilt with him even as his lips claimed hers. It
seemed as if she had been waiting for this
moment all her life, eagerly caressing the tan
broadness of his shoulders and back, knowing
that although Gavin had always kept himself
physically fit he had never attained the lean

fitness that came from working out on a land that made rugged individualists of any men brave enough to challenge it. Kyle Whitney was such a man.

Kyle looked down at her as if suddenly sensing another man partly held her attention. 'Do you want me to stop?' he rasped.

She knew that if she said yes then he would end this right now, but she didn't say yes, her answer much more tangible as she curved one hand about his nape and brought his mouth down to hers.

Kyle's hands touched her everywhere, the curve of her breasts, the slope of her waist, the soft mound of her womanhood, pushing one of his legs between hers to allow him greater access to the latter, caressing her until she gasped for fulfilment.

He was a master in the art of a woman's body, sought out pleasure spots she hadn't even guessed that she had, the curve of her spine knowing the rasp of his tongue as she squirmed beneath him in ecstasy, their bodies glowing deeply in the glow from the fire, the injury to Shelby's ankle forgotten—by both of them.

But she wanted to touch him too, wanted to know what gave him pleasure, pushing him down beneath her to explore every muscled sinew of his body, feeling elated satisfaction as he shuddered and groaned his own pleasure in her touch.

He could stand her torment no longer, pulling her on top of him, moving her hips erotically over his but still not making that final thrust that would join them together in total unity.

Shelby felt a heady sense of power in her dominant position, teasing him with the promise of her mouth but denying him more than fleeting butterly kisses that gave him no satisfaction at all, her hands light on his body as she caressed him, her breasts temptingly only inches from his face.

It was so easy to forget who they were and where they were as Kyle lay her beneath him, his hair-roughened thighs between hers as he probed the intimacy of her body with unerring accuracy. He filled and possessed her completely, adjusting to the demand of her body before moving slowly inside her, each thrust deeper than the last, an unfamiliar warmth invading Shelby's lower body, spreading outwards and inwards, spiralling out of control as Kyle touched her hardened nipples with the warmth of his mouth at the same time.

Her gasp of surprised pleasure was quickly followed by Kyle's throaty groan as he joined her on the plateau of ecstasy before they both floated slowly back to earth.

Shelby had never known such true oneness, wanting to share her heady pleasure with Kyle.

But he moved away from her to lie at her side, his arm still about her as he put her head on his shoulder, seeming disinclined to talk as she turned to look at him, all passion gone from his face as he stared sightlessly up at the ceiling.

Her joyous words of a shared intimacy died in her throat at his remote expression, resting her head back on his shoulder to blink back her tears. Kyle couldn't have told her any more clearly that although he had enjoyed what had just happened he would have wished it had been with any other woman but her.

She gave a pained cry of protest as he got up to leave her, unknowingly provocative as she leant up on one elbow to watch him, her breasts aroused and inviting even now.

'So we don't freeze to death,' he told her dryly

as he placed his own quilt on top of them before joining her again.

Shelby snuggled up against him once more. 'Kyle——'

'It's late,' he interrupted abruptly. 'I think you should go to sleep.'

'But——'

'It happened, Shelby,' he rasped. 'We can't undo that now.'

She didn't want to, but he didn't seem to feel the same way. Obviously he hadn't felt the same uniqueness to their lovemaking that she had. Not even with Gavin, the man she had been married to for three years, had she known that mindless giving in to the senses. Maybe for Kyle she had just confirmed what he had always thought of her anyway, that any male body would do when she was in the mood for loving.

But if he did feel that way it didn't stop him wanting her again in the night, waking her with the arousing caress of his mouth on her breasts, their coming together swifter this time if no less satisfying to them both.

Shelby felt very cold when she woke the next morning, despite the warmth of the fire and the two quilts, her teeth chattering as she sat up to look about her with eyes that couldn't quite seem to focus. She was once again alone, and her efforts to get up and dress herself only resulted in her falling back against the quilts in heated exhaustion, her legs feeling like jelly.

She was still lying there when Kyle came back into the cabin, his eyes narrowing on her flushed and tousled appearance. 'Shelby . . .?' he queried slowly.

She blinked dazedly. 'I can't seem to get up,' her voice—if it were her voice!—came out rough and raspy, and her throat felt like sandpaper. She swallowed hard, looking up at him with pleading eyes. 'I think I'm going to be ill, Kyle,' she admitted shakily.

He came down on his haunches beside her, his hand resting briefly on her forehead. 'I would say that's an understatement,' he sighed. 'You're burning up!'

'But I feel so cold,' she complained, her teeth starting to chatter again.

He pulled the top quilt up to her throat. 'You have a temperature,' he scowled. 'At a guess I would say you're in for 'flu.'

'I'm sorry,' she quivered, feeling tearful.

His expression softened slightly. 'I'm not annoyed with you, Shelby,' his hand was gentle against her cheek. 'Only with the conditions we find ourselves in that make it impossible for me to get medical help for you.'

'But you said they would come for us today,' she said agitatedly, turning to try and see out of the window. 'It hasn't snowed again?' she groaned her despair, feeling iller by the minute.

'No, it hasn't snowed,' Kyle's mouth was tight. 'With any luck we'll be out of here soon.'

She closed her eyes in relief. 'Thank God,' she sighed.

'Yes,' he agreed harshly. 'I think you should try and get some more sleep now, and maybe you'll feel a little better afterwards.'

She didn't seem to be having any choice in the matter, her lids remaining heavily closed.

'Preferably in the bed,' she heard Kyle say as if from a great distance. 'Shelby? Shelby!' his voice sharpened with concern as he received no answer.

She felt too comfortable to move, too sleepy to answer him, nestling down even further among the downy quilts. She heard him curse, knowing she should make an effort to listen to him if she didn't want him to get angrier than ever. But she couldn't make the effort, groaning her protest as the top quilt was turned back and a cold blast of air hit her body.

'It's all right, Shelby,' Kyle's voice assured her softly as she made a half-hearted attempt to retrieve the quilt. 'I'm going to carry you to the bed now, you'll be more comfortable there.'

She clung to him as he carried her across the room, shivering uncontrollably; sighing her satisfaction as he placed her down on the soft bed and covered her up warmly, asleep almost immediately.

She knew nothing of the rest of the morning, not her delirious ramblings, nor the way that she threw off the covers completely as her body seemed to be on fire. She wasn't aware of Kyle's gentle comforting, or the way he constantly sponged down her body to bring down her temperature. And most of all she wasn't aware of the helicopter circling overhead before it landed.

It was late morning when the helicopter arrived to pick them up, the two men piloting the machine ordered to wait outside while Kyle dressed her. Their expressions were speculative when Kyle eventually emerged with her in his arms, although Kyle didn't seem to notice or care as he sat in the helicopter grim-faced with her cradled in his arms.

The noise of the helicopter engine as they took off penetrated her fever somewhat, so that by the time they reached the ranch she was in a half-lucid state, certainly aware enough to hear Kyle snarling out a barrage of orders to what seemed like an army of people as he carried her effortlessly up to her room.

But those few brief moments of lucidity seemed to have tired her, and she once again fell into a fever-drugged sleep, aware of nothing and no one.

The room was in darkness when she woke, no lamp burning as it usually was, and instead of the scratchy blanket against her body she felt something soft and silky against her skin. It took her several moments of confusion to realise she was no longer at the cabin with Kyle sleeping across from her, to remember that she and Kyle had been in the helicopter, that they were now safe.

And with those memories came the ones of the night she had spent in Kyle's arms, of knowing the full possession of that powerful body. She briefly wondered what they would have said to each other the next morning if she hadn't been burning up with fever. He hadn't wanted to talk when they were still in each other's arms, she had no reason to think he would feel any differently in the clear light of day.

She turned now as her bedroom door softly opened and a slim, middle-aged woman came quietly into the room carrying a jug of water and a glass.

The kind blue eyes warmed with satisfaction as the woman turned on the small bedside lamp and found Shelby looking at her. 'So you're awake at last,' she greeted quietly.

'At last?' Shelby echoed, her voice still rasping.

The woman poured some of the water into a glass before helping Shelby sit up to drink it.

'You've been in a delirium for over three days——'

'Three days!' She looked up in surprise, the water having eased the dryness of her throat.

The woman smiled as she eased her back on to the pillows. 'I know it only seems like a matter of hours to you, but I can assure you Mr Whitney has been most concerned by your prolonged illness.'

'Kenny?'

The woman shook her head. 'I meant Mr Kyle Whitney,' she explained.

And Shelby knew the reason for *his* concern. Her illness had just meant that she had to be an unwanted guest on his ranch for three extra days! 'Of course,' she said stiffly. 'I—er—I don't remember seeing you at the ranch before?' she added enquiringly.

The woman smiled. 'That's because you haven't. I'm Amy Summers, the nurse Mr Whitney engaged to take care of you.'

'Nurse?' Shelby echoed sharply.

'No need to look so worried,' Amy chuckled as she made her more comfortable. 'You haven't been close to death's door or anything—although you did have a very nasty fever for a while. But you'll start to feel better now, and the sprain to your ankle is healing nicely.'

She moistened her lips. 'If I haven't been that ill why did I need a nurse?' It was just something else that put her in Kyle's debt, and she didn't like it.

Amy straightened. 'As I understand it there was no one else available to take care of you,' she dismissed. 'And you have needed constant care the last few days.'

Of course she had, and there was only Helen

Whitney here with Kenny and Kyle, any help she had with running the house employed only on a daily basis. 'It would seem I've been a nuisance to everyone,' she muttered.

'Feeling sorry for yourself is just part of your symptoms,' the other woman sympathised. 'You haven't been a nuisance to anyone, you were genuinely ill.'

She wondered if Kyle could dismiss this latest disaster of hers so casually. 'What time is it?' she asked softly.

'A little after six—in the evening,' Amy smiled at her complete disorientation. 'I understand it was quite some adventure you had to get the fever,' she lightly teased.

Shelby instinctively liked the other woman, grimacing up at her. 'I'm sure Kyle didn't put it that way!'

The older woman laughed. 'What man wouldn't enjoy being stranded for two days in a primitive cabin miles from anywhere with a beautiful young woman like you?'

'Kyle Whitney! Sorry,' she added ruefully. 'But I can assure you there was nothing romantic in our situation at all, most of the time I was terrified.'

'Of the blizzard?'

'Of Kyle!'

Amy laughed again, obviously taking it in good humour. 'I've known Mr Whitney from a distance for several years, I suppose he could be a little intimidating.'

That had to be the understatement of the year! 'Is Mr Whitney at home now?' She knew Kyle usually came back to prepare for dinner at about this time. 'Kyle, I mean,' she explained at Amy's puzzled expression.

'No, he isn't here.'

'Er—How about Kenny?' she asked with a casualness she was far from feeling.

'No, he isn't here either,' Amy shook her head.

'Oh.' She couldn't hide her disappointment, at least needing to talk to Kenny so that they could work out the problems between them. 'Do you know when they'll be back?'

'I couldn't say,' the other woman shrugged.

'Oh well, I could do with a shower and a freshen up before I see either of them.' She frowned. 'I take it I can get out of bed now?'

'Only for short periods, you'll find you still feel very weak. But I think you misunderstood me when I said that neither Mr Whitney is at home. I was told when I arrived here that both of them would be away for several days,' she explained gently at Shelby's surprised expression.

She swallowed hard at this piece of information. Did both Kenny and Kyle consider her so unimportant that they could carry on with the business of running the ranch without feeling it necessary to at least give her some explanation for Kenny's callous behaviour? 'I see,' she moistened her dry lips. 'In that case I suppose I'll have to wait until they return. Do you have any idea when that will be?'

'I'm afraid not,' Amy looked regretful. 'Although I'm sure Mrs Whitney will know. I'm going down now to get you a little hot soup, I'll ask her then. And don't attempt to get out of bed while I'm gone,' she warned sternly. 'We don't want any more accidents. I'll help you to wash once you have a little food inside you.'

In truth Shelby knew she didn't have the strength to get out of bed unaided even if she had wanted to, feeling exhausted just from her brief conversation with Amy. Although she did perk up a little bit when Helen Whitney came back into the room instead of the nurse.

Tall and thin, with a constantly worried expression, Shelby had nevertheless come to like and respect Kenny's mother, liking her forthright manner that could be less cutting than that of her nephew's.

'Amy tells me you've been asking about Kenny and Kyle,' she predictably came straight to the point, although she looked more worried than usual.

Shelby nodded. 'She said they were both away on business.'

'Not on business,' Helen shook her head, sighing heavily. 'I'm so sorry, Shelby. Kenny has done a lot of things in the past that I've been ashamed of, but this is the worst of them all.'

She frowned. Surely the other woman hadn't been told that Kenny had deliberately left her out in the storm? But who could have told her, only she and Kenny knew the truth of her 'wandering off after an argument', and she felt sure he wouldn't have admitted the truth to his mother.

Helen wrung her hands together. 'Kyle was so angry when he found out.'

'Kyle knows?' Her eyes widened.

'I couldn't keep something like that a secret,' the other woman sighed. 'Not from Kyle. I hate to think what's going to happen when he catches up with Kenny.'

Shelby was more confused than ever. 'I'm sorry, but I don't understand . . .?'

'Of course you don't,' Helen gave a tight smile. 'Instead of explaining, as I meant to do, I've been indulging in self-pity. And it's you I should be thinking of, not myself. Four days ago,' the words were forced out of her, 'Kenny ran off with Wendy. Kyle has gone after them.'

CHAPTER FIVE

THE roaring fire in the lounge bore little resemblance to the one she and Kyle had shared at the cabin, and yet Shelby wished she were back there now, that she hadn't had to bear the added humiliation of knowing Kenny had run off with his childhood sweetheart.

Three more days had passed since Helen had told her about Kenny and Wendy, and apart from a brief telephone call from Kyle to his aunt the previous evening they had had no word from him concerning the runaway lovers. Helen had rushed to take the call, and although she related the fact that he had asked how Shelby was he hadn't asked to speak to her. Not that she expected he would want to, he obviously had enough family problems to worry about without concerning himself over her, not the least of them being that Wendy's father was reputedly furious about the young couple going off together the way that they had. He had telephoned the ranch on several occasions, and relations were definitely frosty between the two households.

Shelby couldn't say she was altogether surprised by what had happened, not after Kyle had told her of Kenny's reaction to her being lost, although she would have preferred it if Kenny had been man enough to stay and face her. It was his mother she felt the most sorry for, Helen obviously feeling her son's behaviour as a personal reflection on her, and although Shelby had tried to comfort her she had had little success.

Her own health was improving rapidly. She was still slightly weak from her 'flu, but her ankle caused her the most problems, making it difficult for her to get about. She was managing with the help of the walking-stick Amy had supplied before she left yesterday, Shelby no longer requiring a full-time nurse, although she had no idea when her ankle was going to be strong enough for her to make the arduous journey home. Soon, she hoped. Preferably, she would like to be gone before Kyle returned.

In the meantime she could do little more than sit around, doing for herself what she could, not wanting to be any more of a burden to Helen than she already was, knowing the other woman had enough to worry about already.

'Dinner is ready, if you are,' Helen quietly came into the room to tell her.

She followed the other woman through to the kitchen, the two of them eating together in there, a habit they had fallen into in the absence of the Whitney men, Shelby having protested at Helen treating her like a guest, insisting they save time and effort by eating informally in the kitchen.

Helen seemed more troubled than ever tonight, having no appetite for the delicious beef she had prepared, pushing the food uninterestedly about her plate, her tortured thoughts inwards.

Shelby eyed her worriedly. The other woman really had taken Kenny's behaviour badly, and she was going to make herself ill if she weren't careful. 'Is there anything wrong?' she finally felt compelled to ask.

Helen looked more distraught then ever, looking all of her fifty years at that moment. 'He found them,' she revealed jerkily. 'Kyle found them!'

She put her own knife and fork down slowly, taking her time about answering. 'He told you that yesterday?' she prompted, wondering why she hadn't been told before.

'Yes,' Helen acknowledged shakily. 'That was all he would say, that he had found them. He said he would tell me more about it when he gets back.'

Shelby slowly moistened her suddenly dry lips. 'Kyle is coming home?'

'Yes,' the other woman nodded, her hands moving together agitatedly.

'When?' Suddenly her own hands felt decidedly damp and shaky.

'He didn't say,' Helen said dismissively. 'Just that he would be back within the next few days.'

She swallowed hard, doing her best to look cool and calm. 'And will Kenny and Wendy be with him?'

'He wouldn't tell me that either, said he would explain everything when he gets here.' She looked at Shelby with pained eyes. 'You do suppose they're all right, don't you? Kyle was so angry when he left here that I——'

'I'm sure Kyle won't have harmed either one of them,' she assured with quiet confidence.

Helen still didn't look convinced. 'You didn't see him before he left,' she shuddered at the memory. 'It was just like history repeating itself. Well, almost.'

Shelby looked puzzled, wondering if Helen were all right or if the strain of the past week had been to much for her. 'What do you mean?' she prompted softly.

The older woman was pale now. 'I'll never

forget the day his father stormed out of here after Jim. Of course the circumstances were slightly different, but I'm sure Kyle must be reliving the similarities. Of course, he was only fourteen at the time, but that can be a very impressionable age.'

'Helen, I don't wish to sound dense, but I . . .' she shook her head, shrugging her puzzlement.

'Of course you don't understand,' the other woman sighed. 'It isn't something any of us like to talk about, least of all Kenny. He was still only a baby when his father walked out on us.'

'Jim was your husband?' Shelby finally realised the connection, although not exactly the similarities.

'Yes,' Helen acknowledged bitterly. 'For two years I suppose you could call him that, we did go through a marriage ceremony. But for Jim I'm afraid that was the limit of his commitment. He was never a true husband to me, and he certainly was never a father to Kenny. I doubt if he was ever faithful, and when he and Katherine fell in love . . .!' She shook her head. 'He didn't give Kenny and me a second thought. Neither of them did, they just went.'

Shelby found these disclosures a little awkward, in the circumstances, although she said nothing as Helen poured her heart out. The poor woman obviously hadn't had an easy life, deserted so early in her marriage by her unfaithful husband, and Kenny's behaviour now couldn't be helping. But in view of the fact that Shelby was no longer going to become a member of the family she felt as if she were intruding into a private family matter. Kyle Whitney certainly wouldn't approve of her being told quite so much about his uncle.

But the other woman seemed to need to talk,

and Shelby didn't like to stop her, saying nothing as Helen began to talk again.

'Kenny's resented what he calls the Whitney charity all his life,' she sighed. 'Always looking for a way to escape from it and the past.'

Shelby briefly wondered if marrying her would have been one of these ways of 'escape' he sought. Although it didn't make much sense to her, Kenny and Kyle were partners, so why should he consider living at the Double K charity? There were too many things she didn't understand, and most of all she didn't understand Kenny.

'Well I think he may finally have found it this time.' Helen stood up to agitatedly clear the table, needing to have something to do with her hands. 'I doubt Kyle will take him back here after this latest escapade. It was bad enough when Kenny told him he was marrying you, but— Oh I am sorry,' she was instantly contrite at her thoughtless disclosure, looking pleadingly at Shelby for understanding.

'It's all right, Helen,' she gave a tight, humourless smile. 'I'm well aware of how much Kyle disapproved of me as a wife for Kenny, he made no secret of it.'

'That was before he really knew you. I'm sure that since you've been here——'

'He still feels the same way,' she told the other woman gently. 'Even though there will no longer be a wedding.' She had ordered all the plans for the following week to be cancelled as soon as she felt strong enough to think properly, knowing that even if Kenny could come up with a feasible excuse for his behaviour—although she doubted it!—she could never marry him now.

'I wish you would reconsider that, at least

wait until Kenny gets back and you can talk to him.'

'*If* he comes back,' she pointed out softly.

Helen seemed to look iller than ever. 'He has to come back,' she said worriedly.

Shelby thought the other woman might be being a little optimistic, although she didn't say so. She couldn't imagine why Kenny had left in the first place if he intended coming back. Kyle probably only wanted to find his cousin to find out what they were to do about the ranch.

And she had no idea how she was going to face Kyle when he got back! She had thought a lot about the night they had spent in each other's arms the last few days, and although she would have liked to blame it on the onset of her illness making her act out of character she knew she couldn't in all honesty do so. At the time she had gone into Kyle's arms she had known exactly what she was doing. She wondered what reason he had used to himself to justify his own actions.

When she heard the car drive up to the house the following evening she knew that Kyle was home. And coward that she was she remained in her room when she heard the deep timbre of his voice downstairs, telling herself she was giving Kyle and his aunt time alone together, but knowing that she really didn't feel confident about seeing him just yet.

There was silence downstairs for some time after his arrival, then a couple of doors slammed a short time later and she heard someone coming up the stairs, knowing that if Helen was upset by something Kyle had told her that she should really go and talk to the other woman.

Kyle was in the process of shrugging out of his

suit jacket when they confronted each other across the spacious area at the top of the staircase.

His eyes instantly narrowed on her, icy and enigmatic, deep lines of weariness grooved into the side of his mouth and nose, a tired droop to the wide shoulders he flexed beneath the fitted grey shirt.

Shelby eyed him warily, instantly aware of her own appearance as his gaze swept critically over the pale green silk blouse and fitted black trousers she wore. 'I hardly thought we would be dressing for dinner,' she finally said defensively.

For a moment he didn't answer, only continued to stare at her. 'Unless you feel in the mood for cooking it,' he drawled, 'I doubt if there will be any dinner.'

It was incongruous that they should be talking about such a subject when they hadn't seen each other for over a week, at which time they had parted so oddly. 'Your aunt . . .?'

'Is not feeling well,' he ran a hand around the back of his tired nape.

'Kenny . . .?'

His mouth twisted. 'Yes—Kenny,' he rasped with distaste. 'I take it you want to know where the errant bridegroom is too?'

She flinched at his sarcasm, wondering if she could possibly have dreamt his gentleness the night they had made love; he seemed made out of tempered steel now, his clean-shaven jaw rigid. 'He isn't with you, I take it,' she dismissed coolly.

'No, he isn't,' Kyle rasped. 'And if you want to know more about that I'm afraid you'll have to wait until I've at least showered and changed. I've been travelling most of the day, and I'm damned tired.'

'But——'

'I said later, Shelby,' he repeated, his eyes hardened to icy chips.

Her mouth set stubbornly at his dismissal of her. 'And your aunt?'

He shrugged uninterestedly. 'She's downstairs somewhere,' he sighed.

With a contemptuous glance in his direction Shelby brushed past him and went down the stairs, conscious of his gaze on her for several seconds before he turned sharply and went to his room. Shelby was more concerned about Helen Whitney at the moment, and what Kyle could possibly have said to her to have upset her enough to cause her to slam doors; Helen certainly didn't strike her as the sort of woman to become emotionally upset over nothing. She respected the fact that Kyle was tired, knew he must be to have admitted such a thing, but surely he didn't have to come home and upset his aunt more than she already was.

Helen was in the kitchen, sitting at the table sobbing her heart out, and Shelby's heart instantly went out to her. 'What is it?' she moved to put her arm about the older woman. 'Helen, tell me what's wrong? Kenny isn't hurt, is he?' she added concernedly.

Helen shook her head, making some effort to mop up her tears. 'In some ways it might be better if he were!'

'He's coming home?'

'In a few days,' his mother nodded. 'Although Kyle will never forgive him for this.'

Kyle again. Why should everyone in this household be so intent on pleasing Kyle? Well here was one person who wasn't impressed by his arrogance. 'Why don't you go up to your room and lie down for a while, Helen,' she suggested softly.

'Kyle's dinner——'

Her mouth tightened. 'I'm sure I can manage to cook for him for this one night. After all,' she added lightly as the other woman didn't look convinced as to the wisdom of this suggestion, 'I cooked for him at the cabin for several days, and he managed to survive that.'

Helen gave a wan smile at her attempt to joke. 'Maybe I will go and lie down. You'll find some steaks in the refrigerator, and——'

'I'll cope,' Shelby assured her as she helped her towards the door. 'You just go and rest.'

As soon as she knew Helen was safely in her room she went back upstairs herself, not to her own bedroom but straight to Kyle's. He may be tired, but he wasn't the only one, and it was time he told her what was going on.

Her knock on his bedroom door elicited no answer, and after a brief impatient pause she opened the door and went in. Clothes were strewn about the room, his half-emptied suitcase standing open on the bed. But there was no sign of Kyle. Perhaps he had taken pity on his aunt after all and had gone to comfort her.

She was just in the process of turning to leave when the adjoining bathroom door opened and Kyle stood in the doorway, his only covering a towel draped lightly about his hips.

The insolently appraising look he gave her was meant to cause embarrassment at being caught in his room in this way, but for once Shelby refused to be embarrassed by this man, her gaze cool as she looked straight back at him. 'I wanted to talk to you,' she told him firmly.

'Obviously,' he drawled, putting down the

second towel he had been using to dry his hair. 'But couldn't it have waited until I came downstairs?'

She gave him a disparaging look, stung by his condescending attitude. 'I'm not seeing anything now that I haven't seen before. In fact,' she raised mocking brows, 'I've seen much more of you than this—remember?'

For a moment he looked stunned by her bluntly spoken words, and then he smiled, a relaxed and humorous smile. 'So you have,' he acknowledged. 'Although I'm a little surprised at your mentioning it,' he had to admit.

She shrugged, pleased now that she had chosen to bring up the subject rather than wait for him to do so, knowing that this way she had put him at a disadvantage rather than the other way around. 'Are we supposed to pretend it didn't happen?'

His mouth twisted. 'That would be impossible, wouldn't it?'

'I think so,' she nodded, knowing she would never forget the experience.

His eyes hardened. 'Although I hardly think that one night entitles you to walk into my bedroom whenever you feel so inclined,' he bit out.

This time she couldn't prevent the blush that rushed to her pale cheeks. 'I knocked, you just didn't hear me because you were in the shower.'

'In that case it's customary to wait outside until you are heard.' He threw off the towel and began to dress, untroubled by her presence in the room.

Shelby knew that he was now trying to reassert his authority by putting her at the disadvantage she had denied him earlier. And she wasn't going to fall into that trap, could meet him on an equal footing away from the cabin, where he had obviously had the upper hand. 'I think you've lost weight,' she remarked softly, deliberately personal.

His head snapped up, his eyes narrowing at her assessing gaze on the leanness of his body. 'Maybe,' he rasped. 'And now perhaps you wouldn't mind telling me what you wanted to talk to me about?'

'Your aunt is very upset——'

'Understandable, in the circumstances, wouldn't you say?' He pulled on a navy blue sweater to contrast with the light grey trousers he wore, before moving to comb back the thickness of his hair.

Shelby watched him, her senses heightened from having watched him dress, her body tingling slightly now as she remembered running her fingers through that thick dark hair. 'That's just the problem,' she dragged her gaze back to his hard face. 'I don't *know* the circumstances.'

'Helen didn't tell you?'

'She seemed very distraught, I didn't like to pressure her into telling me anything.'

'Where is she now?' he asked resignedly.

'In her room, resting.'

He nodded. 'I think that's the best place for her.' He looked at her with narrowed eyes. 'How are you at taking shocking news?'

She swallowed hard. 'I can take it.' She could take anything after the last week of trauma and uncertainty.

Kyle shrugged. 'Okay, then. I finally tracked Kenny and Wendy down in Las Vegas.'

'*Las Vegas?*' she repeated incredulously, wondering what on earth the other couple had been doing there.

'Nevada,' Kyle nodded, looking at her expect-antly.

Shelby shook her head. 'Why would they want to go there? Kenny doesn't have a secret gambling habit, does he?' she asked with suspicion.

His mouth twisted into a humourless smile. 'If he does it's news to me, but then so have a lot of other things about that young man been lately,' he added grimly. 'No, the reason they were in Las Vegas is quite simple, in the state of Nevada you can get married with no delay.'

'Married . . .?'

'Kenny and Wendy were married a week ago,' he confirmed harshly.

Kyle had said it would be a shocking announcement, but thinking about it she wasn't altogether sure that it was so surprising. Why else would the other couple have run off together if they didn't intend staying together? After all, this was Montana not London, and the very fact that Kenny and Wendy had gone away together had caused a tremendous scandal in the area.

'Shelby?'

She looked up at Kyle, attempting a relaxed smile, knowing she succeeded in part when she saw the admiration in his eyes. 'It's as well I cancelled all of the plans for *my* marriage to Kenny,' she dismissed.

'You did?'

'Yes. Don't look so worried, Kyle,' she mocked his grim expression. 'After all, this is what you wanted.'

'I'll admit I didn't want you to marry Kenny, but I didn't want it to end this way either.'

'Better now than later,' she shrugged.

'Maybe it wouldn't have ended later.'

She gave a bitter laugh. 'Believe me, it would.' She thought of the real reason Kenny had decided not to marry her, knowing now that whenever he had found out about that would have been the time their relationship ended. Thank God she had told him before they were married!

'I hope you don't mean because of what happened between us at the cabin?' Kyle probed.

She gave him a sharp look. 'No, of course I don't. Although you have to admit I could hardly have married your cousin with a clear conscience after that!'

His jaw set rigidly. 'If I had still believed there was any chance of your marrying Kenny it would never have been allowed to happen.'

She raised auburn brows at his arrogance. 'You sound very sure of that.'

'I am.'

'It must be wonderful to have such control,' she scorned. 'Unfortunately, I couldn't have guaranteed the same,' she derided with sarcasm.

'I wasn't even sure you would remember it had happened,' Kyle bit out. 'You were burning up with a fever pretty badly the following day.'

'Oh I remember it very well,' she mocked. 'I'm certainly not going to hide behind my illness.'

'No, you aren't, are you?' Grudging respect again entered his icy grey eyes. 'A lot of women would have done so.'

'Not me.'

'No.'

'Don't look so surprised, Kyle.' She moved towards the door. 'I'm an adult, and as such I take full responsibility for my actions, whether they be right or wrong.'

'I wonder which you consider that night to be,'

he said dryly. 'Don't worry,' he derided, 'I'm not about to ask for an answer.'

Perhaps that was as well, because her answer could have embarrassed both of them! She didn't look at him as they walked down the wide staircase together. 'I'd like to leave here before Kenny and Wendy get back.' She sensed his critical gaze on her as she moved down the stairs with difficulty, her ankle still troubling her. 'I'm perfectly well enough to travel now,' she said with more confidence than she felt.

'The nurse told me you should rest your ankle for at least another few days.'

Her eyes widened. 'When did you speak to Amy?'

'Before I left, and she was pretty emphatic about how long you should rest.' He gave her a stern look. 'It's only been a week now, and already you look as if you've been doing too much.'

She knew that she still looked pale, but there was no need for him to point out that fact. 'I'd rather not see Kenny again now that I know he's married,' she said stubbornly.

'You aren't going anywhere until your ankle is completely better,' he told her with arrogance. 'And you have only just got over the 'flu.'

'Nevertheless, I'd rather leave.'

'No.'

She looked at him with astounded eyes. 'What do you mean, no? I wasn't asking your permission, Kyle, I was just informing you of my immediate plans.'

'And I said no.'

'You can hardly stop me if I decide to go,' she scorned.

'Someone would have to drive you down to the

airport,' he reminded. 'And without my say-so no one on the ranch is going to do that.'

She knew Kyle would be as good as his word, that if so instructed none of the employees here would lift a finger to help her leave the ranch. 'This is rather a turn-around, isn't it, Kyle?' she scorned angrily. 'From the first day I arrived here you've wanted me to leave.' And she didn't fool herself now that his change of mind had anything to do with the fact that they had made love together.

His mouth was grim. 'It's because I feel that you've been given a raw deal that I don't intend to let you leave here now, when you obviously aren't well enough.'

Shelby felt frustrated by his cool arrogance. 'I believe I'm the best judge of that,' she snapped.

'You're still limping badly despite the help of that stick,' he pointed out bluntly. 'And I doubt your strength has completely returned after you were so ill.'

'Your solicitude is welcome,' she drawled, 'if a little suspect. Are you sure you don't just want me to be here when Kenny returns with his wife so that you can witness my final humiliation?' She looked at him with questioning eyes.

His expression was glacial as he looked back at her. 'Think what the hell you please,' he rasped. 'But you aren't leaving here until I'm completely satisfied you're well enough to do so without collapsing at some airport along the way.'

'And just what sort of test do you intend to give me to ascertain that?' her eyes flashed like emeralds. 'We've already proved that I can function in bed even with a strained ankle!'

The pulse jerking in his jaw was the only sign he gave that his anger had increased. 'At least

YOURS FREE

4 Harlequin Presents®
and a fashion tote

It's our way of introducing you to our Harlequin Reader Service that's so much easier and less expensive than buying your novels retail.

As a subscriber, you'll receive 6 new books to preview every month. Always before they're available in stores. Always for the same low price. Always with the right to return the shipment and owe nothing.

P2TMU

◆▶▶ *FREE BOOKS & TOTE BAG* ◀◀◆

YES, please send me 4 **FREE** Harlequin Presents and my **FREE** tote bag. Then send me 6 new Harlequin Presents each month. Bill me for only $1.75 each (for a total of $10.50 per shipment—a saving of $1.20 off retail price). There are no shipping, handling or other hidden charges. I can cancel anytime. The 4 free novels and tote bag are mine to keep, even if I never buy a book from Harlequin.

106 CIP BA5S

NAME_____

ADDRESS_____ APT._____

CITY_____

STATE_____ ZIP_____

your sharp tongue hasn't suffered this last week,' was the only comment he finally made, further evidence of his intense control. 'Now how about dinner, am I cooking or are you?' he abruptly changed the subject.

But Shelby wasn't so easily distracted, still angry at his high-handed attitude to her leaving. 'Are you sure you wouldn't rather go over to Mrs Judd's for dinner? I believe she's telephoned several times.' That was an understatement, she knew for a fact that Sylvia Judd had telephoned daily for any news of Kyle.

'I know about her calls,' Kyle was obviously aware of her sarcasm. 'I'll talk to her later,' he dismissed.

'That isn't nice,' she taunted. 'Not when she's been so *concerned* about you.'

'Don't be bitchy, Shelby,' he advised wearily. 'I've told you Sylvia is only a friend.'

She stiffened. 'It's really none of my business what your relationship with her is.'

'Isn't it?' he shrugged. 'I'm not so sure about that. Doesn't it interest you to know that I didn't already have a mistress when we went to bed together?'

'Why should it?' she dismissed tightly. 'You made it obvious that you considered me unworthy of any man's attention for more than one night!'

'Shelby——'

'Let's have dinner,' she said abruptly, not wanting to discuss that night any longer. 'I'm cooking.'

He continued to look at her undecidedly for several long timeless seconds, and then he shrugged resignedly. 'We'll do it together,' he finally said.

'There's no need——'

'Don't let's argue about that too, Shelby,' he interrupted, his patience—what there was of it— wearing a little thin. 'I seem to remember we called a truce once.'

'And I seem to remember it didn't last very long!'

He gave a rueful grin. 'Then we'll try harder. At least this time if I become too overbearing you can leave the room if you want to.'

'That's true,' she acknowledged dryly.

In the end they didn't work together too badly, cooking the meal companionably, eating silently as they both seemed lost in thought, although Shelby insisted on clearing away, noticing how strained Kyle was looking by that time.

'Thanks,' he took the cup of coffee she brought him through to the lounge. 'I've been putting it off,' he sighed, 'but I suppose I'll have to call Ben Seymore.'

Her eyes widened as she sat down in a chair across the room from him, crossing one slender leg over the other. 'You haven't done that yet?'

'Obviously not,' he bit out. 'It isn't easy telling a man his only offspring has eloped!'

'No,' she acknowledged softly. 'Maybe you should just leave it until Kenny and Wendy get back and let them go over and explain to her father.'

'I said it wouldn't be easy, Shelby,' Kyle rasped. 'I didn't say I wouldn't do it.'

She shrugged, used to his terseness by now. 'In that case I'll go and check on your aunt while you make your call.'

'You don't have to leave, this conversation isn't private,' he dismissed.

Shelby stood up, smoothing down her blouse

before picking up her stick. 'I want to check on her anyway.'

'Please yourself,' he snapped his displeasure at her determination. 'Although going up and down those stairs isn't going to help your ankle in the least.'

She gave him a sweetly sarcastic smile. 'I'll live with it,' she scorned.

Kyle gave her an impatient look before lifting up the telephone receiver and beginning to dial, effectively dismissing her from the room and his mind.

Shelby made her way slowly up the stairs, wondering if she and Kyle would ever be able to meet without resorting to arguing. She very much doubted it.

Her soft knock on Helen's door received no response, and so she quietly opened it, finding the other woman sleeping quietly on the bed, the exhaustion and worry eased from her face as she slept. It was probably the best thing she could be doing at the moment, things never seemed so black in the clear light of day after a good night's sleep.

Kyle was gone from the lounge when she got back downstairs a few minutes later, and so she cleared away their empty coffee cups, just returning from the kitchen when Kyle came out of his study, his expression preoccupied.

'How did Mr Seymore take the news?' she asked as he seemed disinclined to speak.

'As you might expect—angrily,' Kyle grimaced. 'But he'll get over it eventually.'

She nodded. 'Most fathers find it difficult at first to accept that their daughter has found a man she loves more than him.'

'Did yours?'

'My father died years ago, a long time before I was married,' she answered vaguely, watching as he put on his heavy jacket. 'Are you going out?' she frowned.

He gave a rueful shrug. 'I telephoned Sylvia after I had spoken to Ben, she would like to see me.'

Shelby stiffened at his mention of the beautiful widow, sure that the other woman wanted more than just to see him. 'Does it have to be tonight, I thought you were tired?'

'I am.' He looked no less strained than he had earlier. 'But she said it was urgent.'

'In that case I mustn't delay you any longer, must I?' her voice was brittle.

'Shelby——'

'Have a good time,' she told him lightly, sure that the only emergency Sylvia Judd had was that she hadn't seen Kyle for over a week.

He looked as if he would like to say more, then he swore softly under his breath before striding over to the door. 'Why don't you have an early night,' he suggested harshly, making it more of an order than anything else. 'You're looking pale. And tomorrow promises to be a long day.'

'I may be your guest here, Kyle,' she answered him stiltedly. 'But I'll go to bed when I'm good and ready.'

His mouth twisted at her stubbornness. 'I thought you might say that.'

'Then why bother?'

'Force of habit, I guess,' he shrugged. 'I'm not sure what time I'll be back, so I'll see you in the morning.'

'Probably.'

'Shelby, why are you being so difficult?' he sighed. 'I'm only going to see a friend.'

'I'm not being difficult, Kyle,' her tone was scornful. 'It was just that you said you were tired.'

'And now I have to go out and see Sylvia, all right!'

'Fine,' she answered carelessly.

'Oh hell!' he swore viciously before slamming out of the house, the truck roaring away from the house seconds later.

Shelby's breath left her in a pent-up sigh. It promised to be a long night for her, too, if Kyle did but know it. When he had mentioned going to see the other woman she had wondered at her feelings of anger, but as they continued to talk the reason for her almost violent emotions had become clear to her. She had fallen in love with Kyle Whitney!

And it wasn't the hesitant, unsure love she had thought she felt for Kenny, this was the sort of love she had never known before, not even for Gavin who she had cared about so much, the sort of love where she wouldn't hesitate to do anything Kyle asked of her, even become his mistress for the short time he wanted her if he asked her to.

But he wouldn't ask her to, because no matter what he said to the contrary he already had a mistress in Sylvia Judd. As Shelby switched off the main light and made her way slowly up the stairs to her room she wondered if he would even come back to the ranch tonight or stay in town with the other woman.

CHAPTER SIX

HER head ached when she woke up the next morning, and she knew that part of the reason for that was that although she had tried to sleep she had stayed half-awake listening for the sound of Kyle's return. It had been after one when she heard the truck outside, and that didn't cheer her at all, Kyle having been with Sylvia Judd for over three hours.

He was out on the ranch when she went down to breakfast, although Helen looked more cheerful this morning, her early night obviously having the desired effect.

'I'm preparing a special dinner for tonight,' she confided in Shelby as they ate breakfast together. 'After all, Kenny and Wendy may not have done this the way we would have wished, but it's done now so we might all as well accept it as fact.'

Shelby smiled, knowing the other woman was trying to probe her feelings about the unexpected marriage. 'I'll help you get the food ready, if you like,' she offered, knowing that it cost her nothing to do so and that it set this woman's mind at rest.

'Would you?' Helen instantly brightened. 'When I mentioned it to Kyle earlier he didn't think it was a very good idea at all,' she added worriedly.

'He'll be all right at the time.' Shelby's smile had faded just at the mention of his name.

It was late afternoon when Kenny and Wendy arrived, Shelby in the lounge resting her ankle after helping Helen all morning, Kyle having been out checking on the ranch all day, not even returning for lunch.

Shelby was far from looking forward to this meeting with the other couple, although she was grateful that no one was going to be a witness to it, and as it had to be faced she intended to be graceful about it.

The young couple looked cold when they came in from the icy wind outside, Kenny not seeing Shelby as he moved to the drinks tray to pour a warming brandy for Wendy and himself. But Wendy saw Shelby almost instantly, freezing in the doorway, her pretty young face flushing guiltily. Although aged twenty the other woman always looked younger, small and delicate, her hair black and silky about her elfin features. She looked as flushed and beautiful as any new bride should at the moment, although the wary look persisted in her eyes, and she nodded her head in Shelby's direction as Kenny handed her the glass of brandy.

He turned expectantly, his own expression becoming wary too now, his shoulders straightening defensively. And he had the blackest eye Shelby had ever seen! It ranged in colour from a sickly yellow, through to purple, and finally black. And it looked as if it had been very painful to suffer as well as to receive.

Shelby was standing too now, slender and beautiful in fitted denims and a loose silk top. 'I believe congratulations are in order,' she drawled.

Wendy looked more uncomfortable then ever, although Kenny seemed unperturbed by the situation. 'Thanks,' he accepted lightly. 'Can I get you a brandy too?'

'Why not?' she shrugged. 'We can drink a toast to your happiness then.'

'Shelby——'

'Don't worry,' she softly assured the younger woman at her pained cry. 'I'm not about to make a scene.'

'Thank God for that,' Kenny handed her the brandy before slumping down into one of the armchairs. 'I think we have enough problems with Kyle and Wendy's father without having to worry about you too.' His handsome face twisted with displeasure at the difficulties he knew there were to come.

Looking at him now Shelby wondered how she could possibly have been taken in by him, even despite the unfailing charm he had always shown her with his boyish good looks. Because beneath that, and now perfectly visible to her, was a young and selfish boy who cared about no one's feelings but his own.

'I believe a father usually expects to be present at his daughter's wedding,' she reproved.

Wendy moved to sit on the arm of her new husband's chair. 'Is Daddy very angry?'

Shelby gave her a sympathetic smile. 'According to Kyle he's furious.'

'Oh,' the other woman said weakly.

'He'll be fine, don't worry,' Kenny assured her airily, drinking his brandy with quiet confidence.

'And your mother?' Shelby reminded quietly. 'Will she also be fine?'

He shot her a resentful glare, his eyes hard. 'My mother only wants me to be happy,' he told her arrogantly. 'And she knows I'll be that with Wendy,' he added callously.

She refused to be hurt that he could dismiss their own expected wedding so easily, having learnt a lot of things about Kenny the last week that she didn't like, the least of which was his selfishness. 'I'm sure you will,' she agreed abruptly. 'Although I think your mother would like to see you now, she's been very worried.'

'I suppose so,' he reluctantly unfolded his lean length and stood up.

'And Kenny,' she waited until he turned back to her. 'I want to talk to you later—alone.'

'What about?' he challenged.

She met his insolent gaze unflinchingly. 'I believe you know what about.'

'No,' he dismissed.

'Kenny——'

'Stay out of this, Wendy,' he ordered abruptly. 'This is between Shelby and me.'

'But——'

'And I don't think we have anything to talk about,' he deliberately interrupted his wife a second time as he spoke to Shelby.

Her eyes had hardened to icy green chips. 'I said we could talk alone, Kenny,' she told him with soft determination. 'But I believe we can discuss this just as easily in front of Kyle and Wendy. It looks as if you've already talked several things over with your cousin already.' Her gaze lingered with deliberation on his black eye.

His face flushed angrily. 'Okay, we'll talk later,' he snarled. 'Although it won't change a thing, I'm married to Wendy now,' he warned.

His conceit—and insensitivity—in thinking that was what she wanted to talk to him about made her burn with anger. 'It might interest you to know that I wouldn't have you gift-wrapped now,' she snapped, angered further by his disbelieving expression at her claim. 'I find your cousin to be infinitely more charming and honest,' she bit out.

Kenny looked startled. 'Kyle?' he looked at her dazedly. 'You mean you and he——'

'I mean nothing of the sort,' she now regretted her angry outburst, knowing she had left herself and Kyle open to speculation. And he wasn't going to like that one bit! 'It's just that I found during our time at the cabin together that Kyle wasn't quite the despot I thought him to be.'

Kenny's insolent gaze raked over her assessingly. 'I'll just bet you did.'

Her face flushed at his sarcasm. 'And just what is that supposed to mean?'

'Nothing,' his mouth was twisted with mockery. 'Although maybe I understand the reason I got this a little better now.' He touched his black eye ruefully.

Shelby stiffened, wishing she hadn't even mentioned Kyle. 'I can assure you your cousin's actions had nothing to do with me.'

'Didn't they?' Kenny challenged derisively. 'Come on, Wendy, we'll go and talk to my mother. I think I'm looking forward to our little chat now, Shelby,' he taunted before following his wife from the room.

She sat down abruptly, wondering what she had done now. If only Kenny hadn't been so sure she still wanted to marry him none of this would have happened! But she doubted Kyle would accept that as a good excuse for needlessly involving him in her argument with Kenny.

The newlyweds left to visit Wendy's father after speaking to Helen, not returning to the ranch for over an hour, although Wendy didn't look too happy when they did get back. Obviously Ben Seymore wasn't willing to forgive and forget just yet.

For Shelby dinner was an ordeal, Helen making every effort to pretend that everything was normal, and Kyle glowering disapprovingly. Wendy was still very subdued, only Kenny seemed his usual effervescent self.

'I take it Wendy and I can stay here until Ben cools down?' he prompted Kyle.

Grey eyes hardened. 'If he ever does.'

'Of course he will,' Kenny dismissed confidently. 'Wendy is his only child.'

'Yes,' Kyle grated. 'It would seem you have married yourself an heiress.'

Wendy giggled at the description. 'I would hardly describe myself as that, Kyle, Daddy's ranch isn't nearly as big as this one.'

He smiled at her, a gentle smile he would normally reserve for a child. 'Nevertheless, it will all be yours one day,' he pointed out softly.

She looked disconcerted. 'I suppose it will. How lucky that I'll have Kenny to run it.'

'How lucky,' Kyle drawled, giving his cousin a hard-eyed stare.

Shelby only half-listened to the conversation, finding none of it to be any of her business now that she was no longer going to marry Kenny. She just wanted to get through what time she had left here and then go. She almost fell off her chair when she heard Kenny's next words.

'Just what did you do to Shelby during those two days at the cabin to get her to have such a change of opinion about you, Kyle?' he asked with feigned innocence.

Guilty colour washed over her cheeks as Kyle gave her a narrow-eyed glare. 'I told you earlier, Kenny,' she said agitatedly. 'Kyle just took very good care of me.'

'You didn't say that at all,' he mocked. 'As I

remember it you said he was charming and honest.'

'So?'

'So I've never known Kyle to be charming to any woman unless he was after a conquest.' He looked challengingly at his cousin. 'How did you do, Kyle?'

His mother gasped at his crudity. 'Kenny——'

'Stay out of this, Helen,' Kyle bit out between clenched teeth, the icy control in his eyes a warning most people would be wise to heed. 'I did the job you should have been doing, Kenny, I looked after your fiancée.'

'Ah, but how did you "look after" her?' the younger man persisted mockingly.

Kyle drew in a controlling breath, his jaw tight. 'Unless you want your other eye blacked I would advise you to watch what you say or imply about either Shelby or myself.'

'This gets more interesting by the moment,' Kenny was unperturbed by the fury he had aroused. 'After being alone together for only two days—and nights,' he added softly, 'you leap to each other's defence at the slightest provocation.'

'Kenny, I think you've said enough,' his mother said firmly. 'If you would all like to go through to the lounge I'll bring through the coffee,' she bravely tried to change the subject to something less inflammatory.

'Not for me, thanks,' Kyle stood up abruptly. 'I have some paperwork to catch up with in my study.'

Shelby watched him go with dismay in her eyes. He was furious, and he had every right to be!

'You'll push him too far one of these days,

Kenny,' Helen was warning her son worriedly. 'And then what will we do?'

'Do?' he drawled unconcernedly. 'Kyle doesn't own me any more, Mother,' he put his arm about Wendy's slender shoulders, his expression one of defiance.

Shelby had the feeling it was time she and Kenny talked now, and then perhaps he could clear up all the things that seemed to be puzzling her. She certainly wanted some answers from someone. 'Could we have that talk now, Kenny?' she suggested stiltedly.

'Why not?' he grinned. 'It promises to be more interesting than I could possibly have imagined. Stay and help Mother with the coffee, darling,' he instructed his wife. 'Shelby and I shouldn't be long.'

'Do you always treat her so arrogantly?' Shelby snapped once they were alone in the lounge.

He shrugged, sprawled in one of the armchairs. 'It doesn't hurt to have an obedient wife.'

'I wouldn't have been one!'

'Oh I know that,' he drawled. 'But the compensations made that unimportant.'

'And we both know what compensations they were, don't we?' she bit out resentfully.

Kenny gave a slow smile. 'Money,' he related without regret.

'Exactly,' she looked at him with darkly accusing eyes. 'That was the reason you just went off and left me to my own devices in that blizzard, wasn't it?'

'Well you have to admit that what you told me had to come as a shock.'

'A surprise, perhaps,' she conceded. 'But I don't see why it should matter to you so much when you own half this ranch,' she gave him a puzzled look.

Kenny looked at her incredulously for several minutes, and then he gave a shout of derisive laughter. 'You mean you still don't know the truth about that? I felt sure Kyle would have told you by now.'

She frowned her puzzlement, thinking over the things Kyle had said about his cousin, none of them enlightening her about the reason for Kenny's behaviour. 'Told me what?' she prompted.

'That the Double K belongs completely to Kyle, that my mother and I are just the poor relations he allows to live here,' he revealed hardly.

Shelby swallowed hard, so many things being explained if that were true. 'But the name Double K . . .?'

'Kyle's parents,' Kenny explained abruptly. 'The ranch was passed down from them to him.'

'Oh God,' she suddenly felt sick. 'Your mother told me you were always looking for ways to escape from here, I was one of them, wasn't I?'

His eyes narrowed to a stormy blue, his face hard with displeasure. 'Just what else has my mother told you while I've been away?' he rasped.

'She talked to me about your father,' Shelby answered vaguely, still untangling the muddle in her own mind. 'About how you were still a baby when he ran off with Katherine.'

'Really?' he grated, looking furiously angry. 'She had no right to tell you any of that.'

'She's been worried——'

'Because I did the same thing?' he scorned

unpleasantly. 'There was no other way I could get Wendy's father to agree to our marriage.'

'But I thought the two of you had been going out together for years before you came to London?'

'We had,' he bit out. 'But suddenly Ben decided it would be better if Wendy finished her education before thinking of a serious relationship. And that could have taken anything up to another five years!'

'And you couldn't wait that long!'

'No,' he sat forward. 'I've lived and worked on this ranch all my life, knowing it was only so because of first Kyle's father's charity and then Kyle's himself,' his tone was vehement. 'I'm not afraid of hard work, and at least ranch work is something I know, but I don't intend to go on working here for ever, knowing that eventually it will be Kyle's offspring that inherit it all. In other words, I'm sick of their charity!'

'I'm sure Kyle has never thought of it as such——'

'There you go again, defending him,' Kenny derided harshly. 'But you aren't the one who's had to live here all these years knowing you were just tolerated, a family obligation.'

'I'm sure your mother never looked at it that way.'

'My mother!' he rasped. 'She thinks that everything Kyle does is wonderful. I just want to get away.'

'So you decided to marry me,' she said dully. 'The rich little widow.'

His mouth twisted. 'Only you weren't so rich, were you?' he dismissed callously.

'As a widow I am!'

'But not as my wife!'

How ironic that she had unwittingly fallen into the trap that she and Gavin had feared for her, that some man, after Gavin had died, would want to marry her for her money and not for herself at all. It had turned out to be just that way with Kenny.

Two years after she and Gavin had been married they had been told that he had a terminal illness. It had been a terrible blow to them both. Gavin had only been forty-four then, far too young to die, and Shelby had been desolate at the thought of losing the man she loved so deeply. But once the initial shock had worn off they had begun to discuss and plan their future, what little there was of it.

They had shocked London society when they first married, Gavin O'Neal the business tycoon marrying the young girl who had been his own sister's manicurist. She had been twenty-one to his forty-two then, and with both her parents dead and no money of her own everyone had believed her to be a fortune hunter. It hadn't been true, of course, she would have married Gavin if he didn't have a penny, had felt cherished and loved by him, a feeling she hadn't known since her happy childhood with her parents. But Gavin's family had gone along with the general opinion that she could only have married him for his money, and it was only Gavin's steely determination that his family and friends should accept her that had made her welcome in their homes.

But the two of them hadn't cared or worried about other people's opinions of their marriage, had enjoyed a quietly ecstatic two years together before they were told of his illness, their time together after that becoming even more precious to them.

There had only been one thing Shelby was adamant about, and that was that she wanted none of Gavin's money once she had been left alone. At his insistence she had opened O'Neal's shortly after their marriage, the salon attracting the rich and the famous, and she didn't want any more than that from him, knew that would only convince all the cynics that they had been right about her motives in marrying him. But Gavin had been just as stubborn, insisting that as his widow she was entitled to all that he had. She hadn't wanted or needed it, had desperately tried to think of a way to convince him that she didn't want his money. Finally he had taken pity on her dilemma and agreed to the suggestion that she now knew had made Kenny change his mind about marrying her. While she was Gavin's widow his millions would remain hers, as he wanted them to, but if she ever did decide to marry again—and Gavin had insisted that she should, that she was too young to be alone for the rest of her life—then the money would revert back to his two sisters.

She had informed Kenny of that provision in Gavin's will the evening before the blizzard, believing it would be unimportant to him when he was obviously so rich himself. She had soon learnt how wrong she was about that, once he had got over the shock he had dropped her so quickly it had left her breathless. It wasn't even as if she were penniless, O'Neal's would keep her in relative comfort for the rest of her life, in fact she hadn't touched a penny of Gavin's money since his death. But what would still be hers once she married Kenny obviously hadn't been enough for him; Wendy had proved to be a much more profitable prospect when he considered his options.

'No, not as your wife,' she answered him now. 'What a shock that must have been to you.'

'That's an understatement,' he grimaced. 'All those months wasted!'

'Yes,' she snapped. 'And all the time I thought how noble you were being by offering to live in London so that I could continue to run O'Neal's.'

'I have to admit that the idea of living in London did appeal to me, but I can't have everything,' he shrugged. 'The Seymore ranch isn't anywhere near as big as this one, but at least one day it will be all mine.'

'And Wendy's.'

His mouth twisted. 'You've already said it yourself, Wendy does as I tell her. It was something I had to consider when I realised you weren't anywhere near as rich as I thought you were.'

'So you sold yourself to the most amenable of us!'

'Yes.'

'God, I pity her,' Shelby shook her head disgustedly. 'But I'm grateful to her too, I could so easily have been in her place,' she explained insultingly.

Kenny flushed angrily. 'Don't sound so self-righteous, *I* was the one who changed my mind—remember?'

'Yes,' she shuddered at the lucky escape she had had. 'Thank you!'

'My pleasure,' he drawled.

'Maybe,' she snapped. 'But leaving me out in that blizzard was going a little far, wasn't it?'

'I knew Kyle would find you,' he said without remorse.

'You couldn't be sure of that,' she grated. 'It was pure luck that he did.'

Kenny shrugged. 'You're safe now, and from the sound of it the two of you had quite a good time during those two days, so what are you making such a fuss about?'

'Why you——'

'Calm down, Shelby,' he bit out as he warded off her flailing hands. 'Can't you take a little teasing?'

'Teasing!' she glared up at him. 'Your innuendoes about Kyle and myself, when he saved my life, are tasteless!'

'Don't be so melodramatic,' he dismissed.

'I could have died out there, damn you! And how do you think Kyle would react if he knew the real reason you abandoned me?' she flashed defiantly.

'He would probably beat me to a pulp,' Kenny mused in an unworried voice.

Shelby wrenched away from him, just his touch sickening her now. 'You don't seem very concerned at the prospect,' she eyed him with suspicion.

'Because I'm not,' he smiled. 'You won't tell Kyle the truth about that day.'

'Why won't I?' she said with indignation.

'Because you no more want him to know the terms of your husband's will than I do,' he explained confidently. 'Kyle is already convinced you're a fortune-hunter.'

'With a great deal of help—and misconception—from you!' she glared at him.

'True,' he nodded. 'But do you think knowing the details of your marriage, the fact that your husband was very rich and so much older than you, will convince him to the contrary?'

She flushed at his taunt. 'I loved my husband!'

'I'm not disputing the fact,' he shrugged. 'In

fact, having come to know you as well as I do I'm sure that you did.'

'Well, then?' she challenged.

'Do you honestly think the fact that you *thought* you were marrying the *young* and rich half-owner in a cattle ranch will make any difference to Kyle's opinion of you?'

She went very pale. 'I would still have agreed to marry you if I had known the truth about you from the beginning, wealth has never been important to me.'

'Unfortunately it's very important to me,' he drawled.

'I know that now!'

'There's no point in discussing that now, the point I'm trying to make is that Kyle will never believe you're uninterested in wealth. Who do you think he would believe if I were to tell him that was what we argued about that day?' he mocked. 'That I had finally told you the truth about myself and you had walked off. Do you think he would believe your version or mine?'

She was breathing hard in her agitation. 'You know that isn't the way it happened,' she gasped.

'Only the two of us know that.'

She swallowed hard, feeling sick again. 'Why should you want to lie about it?'

His mouth twisted into the ugly caricature of a smile. 'Because something did happen out there between the two of you, no matter how much you deny it. And I'm certainly not going to have you as a cousin-in-law.'

'You needn't worry about that,' she scorned. 'Kyle doesn't think of me in that way.'

'And you?' Kenny's eyes were narrowed. 'How do you think of him?'

She daren't think of him in any way, knew that

with this last threat Kenny had irrevocably closed the door on any hopes and dreams she may have had about Kyle and herself. They had been impossible dreams anyway, Kenny had just made them more so.

She met Kenny's gaze unblinkingly. 'I think of him as the man who undoubtedly saved my life. I'll never forget that.'

'Your gratitude is duly noted—and completely unnecessary,' Kyle rasped from behind them, causing Shelby to turn sharply, her face pale as she knew by the steely implacability in his eyes that he had misunderstood the statement and now imagined she had made love with him out of a sense of gratitude.

How wrong he was about that. If she were grateful to him for anything it was *because* he had made love to her. She had loved Gavin, but they had been friends before they became lovers, had had a deep emotional relationship first, before the physical relationship. It hadn't happened that way with Kyle at all, she had become physically excited by him the way she never had been about another man, had grown to like and respect him after that. The physical awareness was there between them all the time, giving her a feeling of constant excitement, of expectancy. Kyle had taught her to live and love again in a way she had never dreamed of, and for *that* she would always be grateful.

'I decided to join you for coffee after all,' he added harshly as she made no reply. 'I had no idea I would be interrupting a cosy chat between the two of you. Where are Helen and Wendy?'

'All finished?' Helen appeared with a bright smile as if on cue, Wendy following her carrying the laden tray.

'I think we are—aren't we, Shelby?' Kenny taunted challengingly.

She was still shaken by Kyle's unexpected appearance and the wrong conclusions he had jumped to; answering vaguely, 'Yes, we've finished.'

Wendy moved to put her arm about her husband's waist. 'Everything all right, darling?'

Kenny smiled confidently. 'Couldn't be better.'

'I think I'll take my coffee back to the study with me,' Kyle told Helen abruptly as she handed him the cup. 'I still have some things to do.'

'You work too hard,' she chided.

'Possibly,' he rasped. 'But it keeps the tax-man at bay.' He turned on his heel and left the room, not even sparing Shelby a second glance.

'Poor Kyle,' Helen sighed. 'I'm afraid a lot of work has piled up while he's been away.'

'If you're trying to make me feel guilty, Mother,' Kenny drawled, 'then don't bother. Kyle may work hard, but it hasn't been all work the last couple of weeks.' He gave Shelby a sly glance.

She stood up abruptly. 'Excuse me. I think I'll go to my room.'

'But you haven't drunk your coffee, dear,' Helen gave her a worried look.

'I don't think I'll bother after all,' she dismissed. 'An early night would do me more good.'

There was no argument from either Wendy or Kenny as she hurried from the room. But she didn't go up the stairs, instead she went to the back of the house, knocking on the door to Kyle's study before she had time to change her mind.

'Yes?' The door was wrenched open within

seconds, Kyle obviously not welcoming the intrusion.

Shelby moistened dry lips. 'I wanted to talk to you.'

'Oh yes?' He made no move to stand aside and let her enter.

She nodded, determined not to lose her courage now. 'I wanted to explain what you heard me say to Kenny earlier.'

'What I heard?'

'Don't pretend you don't know what I mean, Kyle,' she said impatiently. 'You know exactly what I'm talking about.'

'Do I?' he drawled, standing aside to let her pass him, closing the door before moving back to sit behind the imposing desk, instantly making things formal between them. 'Explain away,' he watched her with narrowed eyes.

'Kenny was making innuendoes.' She gripped her hands together in front of her. 'About the two of us. I was just trying to convince him how wrong he was.'

'After telling him earlier how right he was!' Kyle taunted harshly.

'I didn't,' she defended heatedly. 'He was just being so unbearable, assuming that I still loved him and wanted to marry him.'

'And you don't?'

'No!'

'The deep love you felt for him just died, hmm?' he derided tautly.

'It didn't just die, he killed it!' she snapped. 'Or have you forgotten he's married to Wendy now?'

'I haven't forgotten a thing, neither that or the fact that I'm still considered available.' His eyes were like chips of ice.

'What is it about you Whitney men that makes you think you're irresistible?' she scorned angrily. 'I just came in here to tell you that no matter what you may think to the contrary, what conclusions you may have drawn from my conversation with Kenny, that I *enjoyed* our night together at the cabin.' She blushed at the honesty of her words, could see he was taken aback by them too. 'Now you can draw some more conclusions from that!' she added heatedly, turning to leave the room as quickly as she could with the hindrance of her injured ankle.

She was breathing hard by the time she got to her bedroom, glad of the privacy to hide her blazing cheeks. She hadn't meant to be quite so frank with Kyle, but somehow he had just angered her into it. The way he angered her into most things!

But she wasn't going to lie about that night, and no matter what else stood between them, she had wanted Kyle to know how she felt about it. The fact that her forthright statement still made her blush was beside the point.

She turned sharply as her bedroom door opened quietly, her defences rising as Kyle entered the room, instantly on her guard against any caustic comments he cared to make.

'I gave what you said some thought,' he told her softly, standing just inside the room. 'And the conclusion I came to,' he moved stealthily towards her, his gaze holding hers, 'was that I enjoyed that night too.'

It was so far from what she had been expecting him to say that her mouth fell open in surprise.

He stood in front of her now, the warmth of his body and the smell of the woodsy aftershave he wore reaching out to her senses. 'In fact,' his strong hands clasped her arms, pulling her body into his, 'I enjoyed the experience so much I'd like to repeat it.'

Shelby felt as if all the breath had been knocked from her body, staring up at him with wide eyes as she felt the evidence of his arousal against her thighs, unable to move away from him, unable to speak.

'Say something, Shelby,' he lightly mocked her dumbstruck expression. 'As you have already pointed out, we're both adults, there's no reason why we shouldn't enjoy the time together that you have left here. Is there?' The last was added harshly, as if he still slightly mistrusted her.

He was offering her a brief affair—and she knew she was going to accept the offer with both hands! 'No reason at all,' she agreed huskily, curving her body even more intimately against his. 'Can I tell you now how much I missed you this last week?' She gave a tentative smile.

'Did you?' His lips were at her throat, moving with erotic warmth against the sensitive skin.

'Too much to express in simple words,' she admitted raggedly, quivering with anticipation as his mouth continued to caress her throat and ears.

'Then show me how much,' he invited gruffly. 'Make love to me, Shelby.'

'Your aunt . . .?' she faltered. 'She'll know you haven't slept in your own bed,' she explained at his frowning look.

'It's my house,' he told her arrogantly. 'I'll sleep where I damn well please. Show me how much you missed me!' he repeated roughly.

It took her most of the night to do so, as with the knowledge of Eve she brought him again and again to the brink of fulfilment only to deny him the final pleasure. Finally he took the initiative, as she had known he would, for all of his self-control, and the time until dawn passed in a haze of sensual pleasure for them both.

CHAPTER SEVEN

SHELBY knew that she would hate the impersonality of airports for the rest of her life, watching Kyle with longing eyes as he came back from the airport shop with a handful of magazines for her, unable to believe she was never going to see him again after today.

Five days—and six incredibly beautiful nights—had passed since Kyle had come to her bedroom, and during that time her love for him had just grown, while he continued to show no emotion towards her other than the physical one, and that was a response he didn't attempt to hide from her during the night hours.

Helen must have been aware of the fact that they were sleeping together, but the older woman said nothing to Shelby about it, and she felt sure she didn't mention it to Kenny either. He would have attempted to make her life a misery if he had known of her relationship with his cousin!

And Kyle's and her own manners to each other before they reached the privacy of her bedroom at night couldn't be faulted, neither giving any indication that they were more than acquaintances. Shelby had taken her cue from Kyle after the first night, and it had continued that way.

When she had suggested yesterday that perhaps she ought to think about going home now Kyle had raised no objections, had agreed that it seemed a good idea. He had even offered to drive her to the airport himself this morning after making her reservations for her the evening before.

'Here,' he handed her the magazines now. 'Would you like to go and have a coffee until they call your flight?'

What she would really like would be to cry out the misery of parting from him on his shoulder. But she simply nodded her agreement to the idea of coffee. 'That sounds nice.'

Kyle smiled at the way she huddled down in her sheepskin jacket, his arm companionably about her shoulders as they went to the restaurant. 'I should think you'll be glad to get back to the milder English weather,' he teased as the waitress saw them seated.

She felt like screaming at him that she wouldn't be glad to get back to anything in England, that she wanted to stay here, with him, for ever. Longer, if possible.

But she said none of those things, gratefully warming her numbed hands around her coffee mug. 'It's certainly different from here,' she answered noncommittedly.

'I know,' he nodded, shrugging out of his overcoat as she did the same, the restaurant temperature too warm for such clothing. 'I went to university there.'

Her eyes widened at this information. 'You did?'

'I lived in London for four years,' he confirmed.

She knew so little about him, their relationship the last week not allowing for conversations about their respective pasts, most of their contact purely physical. 'Did you like it?' she questioned eagerly.

He shrugged broad shoulders, looking very

handsome in the dark suit. 'As you said, it's different.'

He hadn't liked it, she could tell, her excitement that he might one day visit London again fading as quickly as it had arisen.

He leant back in his chair, totally relaxed, dark and virile. 'I did manage to make some good friends during my time there, though.'

'Really?' Her interest sparked again. 'Do you ever visit them?'

'Rarely,' he dismissed with a shake of his head. 'It's over ten years since I lived there.'

Ten years, when she had still been at school. 'That is a long time,' she said dully.

'Yes,' he acknowledged. 'But if I should ever happen to be in London again maybe I'll look you up.'

For another affair? Probably. But she wasn't proud, she would accept any crumb he cared to throw. 'I'd like that,' she nodded, knowing it was probably as remote a possibility as it snowing in August in England. But it was better than nothing!

'I'm sorry things didn't work out for you here,' Kyle suddenly said softly. 'You and Kenny weren't right for each other, but I'm sorry you were hurt.'

The disillusionment she had suffered over Kenny was nothing to the pain of having to leave Kyle. But she knew he wouldn't thank her for saying so, that he wanted to keep their own relationship in perspective. And it had been no more than just another affair to him.

'I'll get over it,' she was talking about him, not Kenny. 'I——' the words became frozen in her throat as she heard her flight being announced, her panicked gaze flying to Kyle's face. His expression, as usual, gave away none of his feelings. 'I'd better go,' she said abruptly.

'Yes.' He stood up to help her back on with her coat, his touch impersonal.

They didn't speak as they walked towards the departure area, Shelby trying desperately to hold back the tears, knowing Kyle wouldn't appreciate such a show of emotion from her.

They stopped a short distance away from the departure desk, Shelby giving a bright smile as she looked up at the man she loved with all her heart. 'Thank you for driving me to the airport,' she murmured huskily. 'I know how busy you are, and I—I appreciate it.'

He nodded. 'Have a good trip home,' he told her abruptly, his expression harsh.

'Don't work too hard, will you,' she said lightly.

'Or you.'

Their conversation was becoming more and more strained, and as the final call for her flight was made she knew she would have to go, taking her ticket from her bag. 'Don't worry about me,' she dismissed. 'I've just had a holiday, remember.'

'Some holiday,' he drawled.

'Yes,' she agreed abruptly. 'Well—goodbye,' she held out her hand to him, not quite knowing how to take her departure from him now that the time had come. She had never been a man's mistress before!

Kyle took hold of the proffered hand, using it to pull her forward into his arms. 'I think we can do better than that, don't you,' he murmured before his head bent and his mouth claimed hers.

It was like being given a short reprieve after

facing the hangman, and dropping her handbag at her feet she flung her arms about his neck, encouraging him to deepen the caress, uncaring of the people moving past them to the desk. Kyle didn't seem too concerned about appearances either, crushing her against him, his tongue moving between her teeth in an erotic message of need. Shelby sighed into his mouth, wishing they could go back to the ranch now and fulfil that need.

But already Kyle's mouth was leaving hers, although his arms remained firm about her. 'Maybe I'll make that trip to London soon,' he said gruffly.

'I wish you would.' She was sure her heart must be in her eyes, but she just couldn't help it.

His dark gaze searched the paleness of her face. 'Do you really mean that?'

'Yes,' she breathed. 'Oh yes!'

'Then perhaps I could——'

'I'm sorry to—er—interrupt you,' the man who had been standing at the desk a short distance away cut in apologetically. 'But if either of you intends to be on this flight I'm going to have to ask you to go through, they're boarding now.'

'Thanks,' Kyle nodded to the man, the moment of intimacy gone as he released Shelby. 'I hope you have a good flight to Washington,' he rasped.

'I—I'll call you and let you know I arrived safely in London, shall I?' She looked up at him with pleading eyes, still feeling the taste of him on her lips.

'Do that,' he invited abruptly.

'Er—Miss, I really do think . . .'

'Yes,' she turned to smile blindly at the hovering man. 'Thank you.' She couldn't quite

meet Kyle's gaze as she looked up at him.
'Goodbye,' her voice was gruff.

'Goodbye, Shelby.'

She daren't look around as she picked up her
bag and walked into the lounge, knowing she
couldn't let Kyle see the tears on her cheeks,
walking straight on to the waiting plane, the last
to board, feeling numb as she strapped herself
into her window seat, turning to look frantically
out of the window for one last glimpse of Kyle as
the plane began to move towards the runway.

She thought she was going to be disappointed,
and then she saw him, leaning against the side of
the truck as he watched the plane's departure
with narrowed eyes. He couldn't see her in the
small window, she knew that, but she could see
him, and her lips silently formed her love for
him.

'Your husband?'

She turned sharply to look at the woman seated
beside her 'Er—no, just a friend.'

The woman nodded understandingly. 'Sometimes I think that's worse.' She leant forward to
look at Kyle. 'Handsome devil,' she murmured
appreciatively.

'Yes, yes, he is,' Shelby agreed as the plane
rose higher and higher and Kyle became smaller
and smaller, until she could no longer see him at
all. Her throat ached from holding in the tears,
and as the woman at her side continued to talk
through the whole of the short internal flight she
wished she had never entered into the conversation, needing to be alone in her misery.

The flight on Concorde from Washington to
London was even more miserable, despite the
shortness of the flight, and the rain falling as she
left the airport didn't help her mood in the least.

The transition from the wilds of snow-covered Montana to the rush and bustle of London made her feel a little disorientated during the taxi-ride to her home, her complete and utter unhappiness not helping the situation.

Her luxurious apartment seemed cold and unfriendly, despite the central heating and the obvious comfort of the furnishings. But she knew it wasn't London or her home that was making her feel so tearful, it was the fact that Kyle wasn't here to share them with her. He was probably already looking on her as no more than a nuisance that had turned into a pleasant memory.

It was too early to call the ranch yet, having missed part of the morning's work driving her to the airport Kyle would be out on the ranch working now. She would rest on the bed for a while and call when she knew he would be at home.

'For a while' turned into several hours, and she woke groggily, the time difference she had experienced from the flight putting her whole system out. It took her a few minutes to gather her thoughts together enough to remember to call Kyle, and she dialled the number with a hand that shook slightly from nerves.

Helen answered the call. 'It's a very good line, isn't it, dear,' she said lightly when she realised who it was.

'Very good,' Shelby agreed abruptly.

'Did you have a good flight?'

'Yes. Helen——'

'What's the weather like?'

She could still hear the rain beating steadily against the window. 'Wet. Helen, is——'

'That must have come as a bit of a shock after the extreme cold out here.'

'Yes, it is. Helen, is Kyle there?' she at last managed to get out forcefully, knowing the other woman was only being polite, but needing to talk to Kyle.

'Not at the moment, no. And Kenny and Wendy have gone out to dinner.'

She wasn't at all interested in the whereabouts of her ex-fiancé and his wife, wouldn't have wanted to talk to either of them even if they had been at home. 'Do you know what time Kyle will be back?' She could always arrange to call again later, knew she wasn't going to sleep any more tonight anyway.

'He doesn't confide his comings and goings to me,' Helen replied gently. 'He could be very late.'

Shelby frowned at this, doing a mental calculation, realising that at the ten o'clock at night it was at the ranch Kyle couldn't possibly still be out working; it had been dark for hours. 'Kyle has gone out for the evening,' she realised dully, realising who he had probably gone out *with* too.

'Sylvia telephoned——'

'Could you just tell him I called to let him know I arrived safely,' she cut in harshly, not wanting to hear about Kyle and the other woman.

'Shelby, dear——'

'I told him I would,' she interrupted again, feeling as if she were slowly dying inside. She had only been gone a few hours, and already Kyle had gone to see his former mistress!

'Shelby, I'm sure Kyle going to see Sylvia isn't what you think it is,' Helen told her softly. 'He just keeps an eye on the business side of her life since her husband died.'

'Kyle explained all about his relationship with Sylvia,' she bit out tautly.

'There you are, then,' Helen said with obvious relief. 'Why don't I take your telephone number and leave a message for him to call you when he gets in?'

The thought of him telephoning her after coming from the other woman made her feel ill. 'It isn't important,' she dismissed. 'This was only a courtesy call.'

'Shelby——'

'I have to go, Helen,' she said brightly. 'It's very late here.'

'But wouldn't you like to talk to Kyle?' the other woman said desperately.

She knew Helen was aware of her relationship with Kyle during the last week, could understand the other woman's feeling of awkwardness at having to tell her he was visiting Sylvia Judd. 'I don't think I'll bother,' she told her tautly.

'But——'

'Thank you for your hospitality the last few weeks, Helen,' she said abruptly. 'Please just give Kyle my message.' She rang off quickly before the other woman could voice any more objections.

Kyle couldn't have wasted any time before visiting the beautiful Mrs Judd. Oh, Helen said that Sylvia had called him, but in the end it didn't really matter who had called who, he was with Sylvia Judd now, and that was what was important.

It hurt her pride as much as anything else to know he had gone back to the other woman so quickly. Hadn't she been woman enough for him this last week? Did he have to go to Sylvia Judd to get the satisfaction in his bed that he needed?

It was no good torturing herself with such thoughts. Her time with Kyle, though brief, had been good for both of them; she refused to think any differently.

Her senior assistant did a double-take as Shelby walked confidently into the salon on Monday morning, and although she dreaded the questions she knew would be coming at her unexpected appearance she knew they had to be faced. She certainly couldn't hide at her flat for ever, although she liked to think that what she had been doing the last three days was resting after her journey. She hadn't let any of her friends know of her return, hadn't felt in the mood for sympathy over the weekend. And if she were really honest with herself she had spent most of the last three days waiting to see if Kyle would return her call in spite of her saying it wasn't necessary. He hadn't.

Her assistant Jenny was a tall willowy blonde in her late twenties, her relationship with a television producer not something she told too many people, mainly because he was already married with two children. Jenny knew he had no intention of ever leaving his wife, and she seemed happy with the situation, called herself a mistress, and didn't mind if her friends knew it.

'Correct me if I'm wrong,' she drawled now, 'but shouldn't you be on your honeymoon?'

Shelby went through to her office, nodding hello to her secretary Sophie as she, too, looked surprised to see her. 'I should,' she confirmed dryly.

'But you preferred to come to work instead,' Jenny derided disbelievingly. 'And just where is your handsome bridegroom?'

'With his pretty bride,' she answered, absently flicking through the mail waiting for her attention on her desk. None of it looked very interesting.

Jenny blinked dazed blue eyes. 'Come again? I thought you just said——'

'I did.' She briefly explained the fact that Kenny was married to someone else, omitting the finer details of their break-up, although that didn't stop Jenny being outraged anyway.

'The rat!' she accused. 'After chasing after you in that shameless way he actually had the nerve to go and marry someone else?'

'Yes,' she confirmed. 'But don't be upset for me, Jenny, I had a lucky escape.'

'If you say so.' But her friend didn't sound completely convinced. 'So it's business as usual?'

'As usual,' she nodded with a smile. 'And if any other good-looking men try to charm me just remind me of Kenny, will you? That should cure me of my romanticism.'

'Will do,' Jenny said lightly, standing up. 'Now would you like to come and check over your establishment? You never know, I could have stripped the place bare this last month!'

Her smile deepened. 'I trust you.' But she walked round with her assistant anyway, feeling her usual pride in the salon as she did so. It was one of the most luxurious and informal salons in London and catered for every need, from saunas and massages to beauty treatment and hairstyling on its three floors. Nothing had been spared on its fitments, the furniture plush and comfortable, the decor warm and inviting, making it more like a place you liked to visit than somewhere women felt compelled to go to maintain their youth and beauty. The whole thing had been Gavin's idea, and he had insisted that if it were going to be done at all it had to be done properly, in style. O'Neal's was a credit to his planning and business brain. It had also become her salvation after his death.

With a business to run, people relying on her for their livelihoods, she hadn't been able to give in to the despair that had engulfed her when Gavin died, had had to carry on for the sake of the people who depended on her. And if it could do that for her once it could do it again, would be the incentive she needed to get her over Kyle.

But that was easier said than done, and over the next few weeks she knew she wasn't succeeding in putting Kyle from her mind, that no matter how much she had worked herself to the point of exhaustion he was never far from her mind.

'For goodness' sake slow down,' Jenny advised worriedly after watching five weeks of this frantic activity, of seeing Shelby get thinner and paler from the pressure of work she put herself under, and the constant round of parties she attended in the evenings. 'It will all still be there tomorrow, you know,' she added lightly, Shelby still working at her desk when everyone else had gone home for the evening.

Shelby's eyes had lost their sparkle the last few weeks, although her smile was just as warm. 'I'll be leaving in just a few more minutes.'

'Promise?'

'What are you going to do if I don't?' she teased.

'Sit right here and wait for you,' Jenny told her stubbornly.

'Then I promise,' she nodded. 'Isn't Don waiting for you outside?' she prompted lightly as the other woman still hesitated about leaving.

'Are you sure you'll be all right here on your own?'

'Very sure.'

'He isn't worth it, you know,' Jenny suddenly told her huskily.

She blinked her puzzlement, feeling more tired than she cared to admit. 'Who isn't?'

'Kenny Whitney!' her friend said forcefully. 'I didn't like to tell you before, but he was still seeing Anne for some time after he started dating you too.'

Shelby blushed at just how gullible she had been where Kenny was concerned. 'I wish you had told me, Jenny,' she sighed. 'Maybe then I wouldn't have been such a fool over him.'

'You seemed so happy with him, I didn't want to ruin things for you.'

'Well don't worry about it now, it's all over,' Shelby assured her. 'And I promise I shall be leaving here as soon as I've added up this last row of figures. All right?' she prompted softly.

'All right,' Jenny nodded.

As she continued to sit in her office after Jenny had left, the salon strangely quiet and eerie now that it was empty for the night, she wondered what Jenny would say if she knew it wasn't Kenny she was missing at all, that it was his cousin she ached for.

She left the salon late each evening, joined in London's constant social whirl until the early hours of the morning, and still she ached for Kyle when she fell into bed each night. Time, she kept telling herself, all she needed was time. But in her worst moments of despair she wondered just how much time.

It was another half an hour before she stood up to leave, the ornate clock on the wall telling her it was after eight now. She swayed slightly as she turned to get her coat, clutching on to the side of the desk to stop herself falling, realising that Jenny was right to be worried about her, that she had been overdoing it. Maybe she would give the party a miss tonight, have an early night for a change and get some rest.

But she felt better by the time she had driven home, put the feeling of giddiness down to the fact that she hadn't eaten dinner yet. The maid who came in every day to clean the flat for her had left her a meal in the oven, and for once Shelby decided not to throw it out but to actually eat it. Trying to forget Kyle was one thing, killing herself doing it was something else entirely. She just wasn't the suicidal type.

It was almost ten o'clock by the time she arrived at the party, and as had become usual with her nowadays she flung herself into the exuberance of dancing the night away, wearing her constant stream of partners out while still remaining full of energy herself.

Quite how she came to find herself lying in a hospital examination room she didn't know, but the stark white decor and numerous instruments attached to the walls meant it couldn't possibly be anything else.

'Lie still,' a middle-aged man in a white coat moved forward to order as she went to sit up, having been standing behind her until that moment.

She did as instructed, frowning deeply. 'What am I doing here?'

'Getting the first rest you've had in weeks, I should think,' he answered sternly, leaving his notes on the desk to come and stand beside the examining couch, tall and grey-haired, with blue eyes that looked as if they could twinkle merrily in the right circumstances, although at the moment they were as censorious as the rest of his features. 'What were you trying to do?' he added angrily. 'Set some sort of record for stupidity?'

Shelby dazedly put a hand over her eyes. 'How did I get here?' she asked gruffly.

'Some of your friends brought you in after you fainted at a party. Although if they were true friends they wouldn't have let you get into this state in the first place,' the doctor bit out. 'You're undernourished as well as suffering from acute exhaustion.'

'I had dinner,' she defended weakly.

'Congratulations!' he quipped with sarcasm. 'There are easier and more effective ways of getting rid of an unwanted baby, you know,' he rasped.

If Shelby had any colour in her cheeks she knew that she lost it at that moment, her mouth opening wordlessly. '*Baby?*' she finally managed to squeak out between numbed lips.

The doctor's expression changed at her complete bewilderment, softened, and she finally saw some of the warmth in the blue eyes she had known could be there when he wasn't so angry. 'You didn't know, did you?' he realised huskily. 'I felt sure that you must be aware of your condition.'

Her 'condition' was still a deep shock to her, too much so to actually be taken in at this moment. 'You've already said I could win prizes in stupidity,' she said weakly.

'That was when I thought—I owe you an apology,' he sighed. 'The way your friends said you were behaving, working too hard, playing too hard, I felt sure you were trying to abort the baby.'

She gasped at that. 'I haven't—have I?' she added in desperation.

'No, you haven't, so just calm down,' he told her kindly. 'Your blood pressure is high enough already without that,' he informed her dryly.

'How——' she moistened dry lips. 'How long? I mean, how many weeks am I?'

He shrugged. 'About six or seven I would think. I was hoping you might be able to help me out a little on that,' he teased.

'Seven,' she said with certainty, somehow knowing the baby had been conceived the night at the cabin, her instincts telling her it was so.

'Then seven it is,' the doctor nodded with a smile. 'My name is Stephen Green, by the way, if you feel like hurling abuse at me for my erroneous assumption earlier.'

Shelby looked up at him with tear-wet green eyes. 'I'm too happy at this moment to want to hurl abuse at anyone, least of all you. You are sure there is a baby?' she added uncertainly.

'Very sure,' he confirmed softly. 'But if you weren't trying to lose the baby by your excessive behaviour what were you trying to do?' he frowned.

'Forget its father,' she told him truthfully.

'Your own husband?' His brows rose in surprise at her answer.

She shook her head. 'I'm not married.'

He glanced down at the notes on his desk. 'It says *Mrs* O'Neal here . . .?'

'My husband has been dead for almost two years.'

'Oh.'

She laughed lightly. 'Don't look so worried, Dr Green,' she teased. 'I'm certainly not.'

He looked at her closely, at her flushed and happy cheeks, and sparkling green eyes. 'No, you aren't, are you? Well perhaps you ought to be,' he told her sternly. 'I mentioned the fact that your blood pressure is too high a moment ago, now that is something to worry about.'

She sobered at his expression. 'Is it serious?' she asked softly.

'It can be.' He didn't spare her. 'Unless you take care of yourself and slow down.'

She smiled her relief, having imagined something much worse. 'I intend to——'

'And I mean to see that you do,' he nodded. 'A few days in hospital should——'

'Is that really necessary?' she gasped her dismay at the thought of it. 'Couldn't I rest just as easily at home?' she added pleadingly.

'You tell me,' he smiled. 'Could you? And I do mean complete rest, for several days at least.'

As she told him of her circumstances she could see he was going to agree to her going home.

'What about the salon?' he probed slowly. 'Rest includes no worries.'

'I have a very able assistant who can take over,' she hastened to assure him.

'Then there appear to be no problems, do there,' he said lightly. 'Although I'll have to make arrangements for someone to come in and check your blood pressure.'

Shelby chewed on her lower lip as he helped her sit up. 'Does this mean I'll have to give up work for the whole of the pregnancy?' she frowned.

'That's what this rest will tell us. Could you do it if you had to?'

She nodded. 'I told you, I have a very good assistant. I'm just not sure I could sit about for the next seven months doing nothing,' she grimaced.

Stephen Green smiled. 'You would be surprised at the things you would find to amuse you. Most women react the same way when told to rest like this, but somehow they manage to muddle through it all.'

Maybe 'they' did, and she knew she would too, if it meant keeping Kyle's baby, but she also knew it wouldn't be easy. She had no family to visit her, to help pass the hours, and in the circumstances she knew she couldn't ask Gavin's sisters to visit her. They would be most disgusted!

Her own doctor called on her the next morning, his examination even more complete than Stephen Green's had been, although thankfully her blood pressure was going down. The next thing she had to do was call Jenny and ask her to come round as soon as she had the salon organised.

'I knew something like this would happen,' Jenny fussed as she came into Shelby's bedroom after being let in by the maid. 'I should have made you slow down.'

'Do you think you could have?' she smiled, wondering what Jenny would say when she knew what actually *had* happened.

'Probably not,' the other woman grimaced. 'So how long do you expect to be confined to bed?'

She shrugged. 'They aren't sure about that yet.'

'The longer the better,' Jenny said firmly. 'You need a good rest.'

'You may not feel the same way about this if you have to stay in charge of the salon for the next seven months!' she warned seriously.

'Seven months?' Jenny blinked at the approximated time. 'Why seven months?'

She gave a rueful smile. 'Because that's how much of my pregnancy there is left,' she explained softly, knowing the news would be a shock for her friend. As it had been for her at the time, she hadn't even thought of pregnancy when she was in Kyle's arms. And she felt sure he assumed she was the one taking the precautions to prevent such a thing. After all, he had believed she slept with Kenny.

'Pregnancy . . .?' Jenny echoed dazedly. 'Are you—You're saying that you're——'

'Yes,' she confirmed gently.

'Oh God.' Jenny sat down abruptly in the bedroom chair, obviously badly shaken. 'And Kenny's married to someone else,' she groaned her dismay.

Shelby knew that it was natural, in the circumstances, for her friend to assume the baby was Kenny's, and she felt very uncomfortable as she told Jenny that it wasn't.

'Then who——? No, don't answer that,' she shook her head. 'I, of all people, have no right to pry. Just tell me, are you happy about it?' she looked at Shelby searchingly.

'Ecstatic!' she answered truthfully.

Once the shock had worn off the night before she had been able to realise just how lucky she was to be having Kyle's child. Not many women could know the same happiness when they had lost the man they loved. Yes, she was ecstatic, and she intended to safeguard the baby's welfare no matter what she had to do.

'Then that's all that matters,' Jenny said briskly.

Shelby wasn't so sure that it was, she had a

feeling Kyle would be deeply interested in the growing existence of his child. But she had already weighed up the possibilities of telling him, knew that he would either insist on marrying her, which when he didn't love her would be a disaster, or he would demand equal rights to the child and it would be tugged backwards and forwards across the Atlantic until it didn't know where it belonged. In the end she had decided silence was the best course of action.

Maybe when the child was older things would be different, but for the moment she intended being its sole parent, would love and cherish it as she had its father.

CHAPTER EIGHT

IN the end she was kept confined to her flat for a month before the doctor decided her blood pressure was stable enough to allow her to spend the mornings working at the salon, although she had strict instructions to spend each afternoon resting, and her social life had been curtailed indefinitely.

She was 'blooming nicely' as her doctor put it, was slowly putting on weight, and had turned out to be one of those lucky pregnant ladies whose complexion and hair radiated health. Whether she would still feel this good by the end of the pregnancy she didn't know, but for the moment she glowed.

After her first week back at work she was just tidying up her desk on Friday lunchtime to leave for the day when Jenny came into the room, a worried frown on her face. 'What is it?' Shelby prompted with a smile, all problems washing over her in her ecstatic state of self-satisfaction, none of them seeming serious enough to warrant getting excited about.

'There's a man in the salon——'

'Wow!' she quipped.

'You don't understand,' Jenny glared at her for her levity.

'He doesn't think this is a high-class massage-parlour like the last one, does he?' Her mouth quirked with amusement as she remembered the slightly inebriated man who had come in about six months ago expecting O'Neal's for Women to be able to give him the entertainment he was looking for. Shelby had taken him aside and spoken clearly and softly to him for a few minutes, and he had left a sadder and slightly less inebriated man. 'Because if he does you'll have to handle this one,' she told Jenny. 'I'm on my way to lunch, and then I have an important appointment to go to this afternoon.'

'You're supposed to be resting then, putting your feet up,' Jenny admonished.

'I do usually,' she nodded. 'It's just that this particular appointment can't be put off any longer.' She wasn't looking forward to the meeting with Gavin's lawyers, but it had to be done.

'If you say so,' her friend still looked disapproving. 'But you've only been back at work a week and already you're breaking the doctor's orders.'

'But it's for a good reason,' she smiled.

'That's what they all say,' Jenny frowned. 'I hope you don't intend——'

'The man, Jenny,' she reminded pointedly. 'I doubt if he appreciates being left out there with a salon full of women—unless he is another drunk?'

'He isn't, and he looked as if he could handle the attention,' Jenny said dryly. 'He didn't look as if much could ever disconcert him.'

Shelby felt the first shiver of apprehension down her spine, and her back stiffened. 'Who is he, Jenny?' she asked between tight lips.

'I was hoping you would be able to tell me that,' her friend grimaced. 'I've never seen him before, but he asked to see you. The suit he's wearing was obviously made at an exclusive tailors—with the width of those shoulders it would have had to be!' she added appreciatively.

'And he's as handsome as the devil, very dark and moody looking. The only thing I can fault about him is that he has that same drawling accent as Kenny,' she said with displeasure.

It seemed impossible and yet it had to be! 'Kyle . . .!' she breathed dazedly.

Jenny shrugged. 'He didn't give his name, just asked to see you. I wasn't sure you would want to see him, though, so I asked him to wait. Shelby, is he——'

'The baby's father?' she finished raggedly. 'Yes,' she swallowed hard. 'Yes, he is.'

'Then I don't blame you at all for preferring him over Kenny,' her friend said gently.

'He is also Kenny's cousin, Jenny,' she told her softly.

'Oh dear,' she frowned at this added complication.

'That's one way of putting it,' she acknowledged shakily, glad she was already sitting down. No traumas or upsets her doctor had warned her when he had let her resume work, and so far there hadn't been any. But no one could have foreseen the possibility of Kyle coming here. She looked down at the rounded softness of her body. At twelve weeks pregnant she definitely had a slight bulge to her tummy, but as she had put a little weight on the rest of her body too, perhaps it wouldn't be quite so noticeable to an unsuspecting man. The last thing she had envisaged had been Kyle coming here and possibly *seeing* her pregnant.

'Shall I show him in or shall I try and divert him while you get away?' Jenny asked worriedly.

'Do you think the latter is possible?' she gently teased, some of the shock leaving her now. She had no idea what Kyle was doing in London so soon after saying he rarely visited here, or why he had come to see her when she had been sure it had just been an empty promise, but she *would* see him now that he was here, knew that she had to.

'I see what you mean,' Jenny grimaced. 'His jaw does have a very determined look to it.'

'That's because he is,' she sighed. 'And I'd rather speak to him here than at my apartment. Give me a few minutes, and then show him in, hm?'

'Okay,' her friend nodded, turning at the door. 'And let me say I think you showed infinitely more taste in him than I would have given you credit for after you dated Kenny.'

'Thanks—I think!'

Jenny grinned. 'And if you ever feel in the mood to talk about it I would love to hear how you became involved with that handsome devil.'

Shelby grimaced. 'I'm not too sure how that came about myself.'

Once she was alone she stood up to check her appearance in the mirror. The silky green dress she wore was loose enough not to emphasise her condition while still remaining fashionable, the weight she had gained adding to her attractiveness. Her hair was as long and silky as ever, her make-up impeccable. Kyle wouldn't be able to fault her appearance, for all that he had appeared so unexpectedly.

She was seated back behind the desk when the knock sounded on the door, the flushed and smiling Jenny showing Kyle into the room before making herself scarce again.

Shelby looked at him with hungry eyes, finding he looked every bit as handsome as Jenny had said he did. But his eyes were cold, and there was no smile to the firm mouth. 'Kyle,' she greeted huskily. 'This is a surprise.'

'Just how much of an annual income does this place have?' he rasped without preamble.

She blinked her surprise at this unexpected attack. Whatever she had been expecting from him it wasn't this! 'I don't——'

He came to stand in front of her desk. 'You knew all the time that Kenny had given his family the wrong impression about what sort of establishment you ran,' he accused harshly. 'Why the hell didn't you tell me the truth?'

'Kyle——'

'And I accused you of being a fortune-hunter,' he added disgustedly. 'You're almost as rich as I am!'

Richer, if he took into account Gavin's millions. But she didn't intend him to know about them, knew that O'Neal's had been enough of a shock for him.

'I thought the cab driver had come to the wrong building when he stopped outside a few minutes ago.' His expression was bitter with anger. 'Why didn't you tell me just how exclusive this place is, Shelby?'

'You had already formed your opinion of me,' she shrugged. 'I couldn't see any reason to try and change it.'

'Couldn't see any reason——!' His eyes glittered dangerously. 'Don't you see, this changes everything?'

'I don't understand why,' she dismissed.

'Damn you, you let me think you wanted to marry Kenny because of his position on the ranch, that you pursued him mercilessly. I formed my opinion of you on that basis,' he added with brutal anger.

'Are you angry at the truth or because you were wrong about me?' she asked quietly.

'I'm angry at Kenny for deceiving me in that way, and I'm angry with you for letting him! It was the other way around all the time, wasn't it?' he ground out. 'Kenny thought he would have a meal ticket for life in you.'

'I——'

'That's the way it was, wasn't it?' he demanded forcefully.

'Yes, it was,' she was as angry as he now. 'Does knowing that make any difference?'

'To what?'

'To anything?' she snapped. 'Of course it doesn't,' she answered her own question disgustedly. 'But if you must know the finer details of our relationship Kenny finally decided he preferred the lure of working on a ranch that would eventually become his rather than be dependent on his wife's earnings. There, does that satisfy you?'

He shook his head. 'I knew Kenny was some things, a lousy son being one of them, but I never dreamt he would go that far! Why didn't you just expose him for the callous young bastard that he is?' His eyes were narrowed suspiciously.

Because it would have meant revealing details about her marriage to Gavin that Kenny had already threatened to distort to suit his own purposes! 'Would you have believed me?' she queried instead.

Kyle's expression was grim. 'Oh yes, I would have believed anything you told me about him after he left you out in the blizzard. No man with any sense of feeling would have done that if he truly cared for you, even if the two of you had argued.'

She turned her head away, wishing she could tell him everything, but knowing she wouldn't even if she could. The evidence against her, knowing Kyle's suspicious nature as she did, was too strong. And then there was the baby. She paled at the thought of what construction Kyle would put on the existence of his child. Probably he would decide she was out to catch herself a rich and not-quite-so-young owner of a cattle ranch!

'Shelby?' His face darkened with concern at how pale her cheeks had become.

'I'm all right,' she assured him, although she knew that she wasn't. This was definitely one of the shocks or traumas the doctor had wanted her to avoid! She rang through for Sophie. 'Could you ask Jenny to come in, please?' she requested tightly of her secretary.

'Shelby, what is it?' Kyle demanded roughly as he sensed something was seriously wrong, coming around the desk to stand beside her, the pleasant smell of his aftershave and the warmth of his body causing her hands to shake. 'Are you ill? Shelby, tell me what's wrong!'

'Get away from her!' Jenny ordered angrily as she stormed into the office, not at all daunted by the fiercely arrogant glare Kyle gave her at her audacity, intent only on protecting Shelby. 'How dare you come here upsetting her?' She pushed him out of the way, her anger increasing as she saw how ill Shelby looked. 'Just what do you think you're doing?' She turned on him furiously. 'Can't you see she isn't well?'

'She looked fine to me until a moment ago——'

'Well look at her now,' she snapped. 'I hope you're proud of yourself.'

'Now just wait a minute——'

'No, *you* just wait a minute,' she bit out between clenched teeth. 'Haven't your family already done enough to her? How dare you come here and upset her again?'

Shelby knew by the angry glitter in Kyle's icy grey eyes that Jenny had far surpassed the outspoken way in which anyone had spoken to him before. But she silently thanked her friend, knew she didn't have the strength to stand up to him herself.

Kyle bit back any more angry retorts he might had made after glancing down and seeing Shelby's chalk-white face. 'Maybe you should see to your patient instead of ranting and raving at me,' he rasped, turning away from them to look out of the window, his hands clenched behind his back.

Jenny shot that broad back a look of pure dislike before bending protectively over Shelby. 'I'll get you home, shall I, love?' she prompted gently.

She nodded. 'And could you call my three o'clock appointment and tell them I can't make it, you'll find the number in my book.' She looked pleadingly at her friend, not wanting to discuss the identity of that appointment in front of Kyle.

Jenny glanced down at the book, her brows rising as she recognised Gavin's lawyers. 'I'll do that,' she promised. 'After I organise a taxi to take you home.'

'I——'

'No arguments, Shelby,' she told her sternly. 'You aren't in any condition to drive, and you know I can't.' She turned to look at the rigidity of Kyle's back. 'And don't you dare bully her while I'm gone,' she warned him.

The only indication he gave that he had heard

her was the slight stiffening of his back, turning slowly as the door closed behind Jenny. 'Just what the hell did you tell the woman about me?' he ground out. 'I get the feeling Attila the Hun would have got more of a welcome than I did!'

She couldn't help smiling at that. 'Jenny is just very protective.'

'That has to be an understatement!' he frowned. 'What *did* you tell her about me?'

'Until you arrived here a few minutes ago absolutely nothing,' she answered truthfully. 'Until then she wasn't even aware of your existence.'

'I'm not sure if that's a compliment or an insult?' he drawled. 'I didn't even merit a mention during one of your girlish chats over a cup of coffee?'

'No.'

'I thought all women liked to discuss whether or not the man in their life was a good lover.'

She flushed at his derision. 'You aren't the man in my life any more. And Jenny and I don't have those sort of chats,' she dismissed. 'I certainly didn't tell her any details about you.'

'Why not?'

She shrugged. 'Our relationship isn't the sort of thing I usually discuss with my friends.'

'Our affair, you mean?' he bit out.

'A week together hardly merits that description,' she derided. 'You never did say what you're doing here, Kyle?' she prompted, feeling a little better now.

'I came over on business. And I did say I would call on you if I was ever in London.'

'So you did,' she acknowledged brittlely. 'I just didn't think that day would ever come.'

His mouth twisted. 'Sorry to disappoint you.'

'Oh, I'm not disappointed,' she assured him hastily. 'Just surprised, as I said earlier. When do you expect to return to Montana?'

'I only arrived yesterday,' he derided.

'Oh.' That really did surprise her, she wouldn't have thought he would have found the time to come and see her so quickly. 'Do you have somewhere to stay?'

'Well I didn't sleep on a park bench last night!'

She flushed at his mockery. 'I was only being polite, Kyle.' And trying to find out which hotel he was staying at!

'Don't worry,' he taunted. 'I didn't come here expecting to stay with you.'

She met his gaze unblinkingly. 'You could have done, I have a spare room.'

His eyes hardened at her pointed reference to separate sleeping arrangements. 'And wouldn't the "man in your life" find that a bit strange?'

She knew he was referring to the fact that she had claimed *he* was no longer that man. She toyed with the idea of lying to him, and then dismissed it. She certainly wasn't going to be reduced to playing those childish games to protect herself from the love she still felt for him. 'There is no man,' she told him bluntly. 'And if you had told me you were coming I could have got the spare room ready for you.'

'It was a last-minute business decision. And I'm not sure I would have presumed on your hospitality even if I had thought of it. You're different here,' he spoke slowly. 'More remote.'

Remote, when all she really wanted to do was throw herself into his arms! But she daren't even let him that close, knew the intimate contact would make him aware of the changes in her body since he had last held her. She had to keep her distance, but at no small cost to herself.

'This is my world, Kyle,' she shrugged. 'I'm bound to seem different here. And Montana is your world.'

'In other words, you would rather forget what happened between us there, wish that I hadn't come here to see you?' he bit out forcefully.

'That isn't the way I feel at all,' she snapped. 'In fact, I was just about to invite you over for dinner tonight.' She heard herself make the suggestion with dismay. She should have just let him walk out of here with the intention of never seeing her again; this way she had exposed herself to her secret being discovered.

'Tonight?' he questioned sharply.

'Yes,' she nodded, not willing to back down now that she had made the offer.

His gaze raked mercilessly over her face. 'Are you sure you're well enough for entertaining?' he rasped.

'I will be by tonight,' she nodded with confidence, knowing that a few hours' sleep and she would be herself again.

Kyle frowned deeply at that. 'What's actually wrong with you?' he asked slowly.

She could feel her face blushing her guilt. 'After my month away,' she spoke quickly, 'there was a lot of work to catch up on. I overdid it.'

'You seem to have a habit of doing that,' he derided. 'I don't——'

'Taxi's here,' Jenny came in to cheerfully announce, looking questioningly at the two of them as they fell silent. 'Everything all right?'

'I haven't taken advantage of your absence to beat Shelby into submission across her desk, if that's what you mean,' Kyle was the one to answer her, walking confidently to the door. 'And for your information,' he looked down at Jenny with mocking eyes, 'I don't bully Shelby, she manages to give out as good as she gets. Better sometimes.'

'Good,' Jenny smiled.

He grinned back at her. 'I'm glad you think so.'

'Kyle——'

'I'll see you later, Shelby,' he told her softly. 'And don't worry about dinner, I'll bring it with me.'

'Just what did he mean by that?' Jenny asked suspiciously once he had left.

She gave a rueful shrug, knowing she was in for an argument. 'I've invited him over for dinner tonight.'

'You've done *what*?'

She sighed. 'Jenny——'

'You're in no condition to give him dinner or anything else!'

She laughed at the latter. 'I didn't intend giving him "anything else".'

'You're going straight home to bed and staying there,' her friend told her determinedly. 'You certainly aren't getting up later to cook his dinner!'

'You heard Kyle, he'll do it.'

'He said he would *bring* it,' Jenny corrected impatiently. 'That isn't the same thing at all.'

'I can assure you that he's a very good cook,' she teased.

'I don't care if he's Cordon Bleu, you had no right to invite him over tonight.'

'At least this way you'll be certain I've eaten,' she reasoned.

'I can always be sure of that, I had a word with

your maid weeks ago to make sure she left you a good meal.'

'She told me,' Shelby nodded.

'I'm beginning to think you and this Kyle deserve each other!' Jenny said at her stubbornness.

She was smiling openly now. 'I'm sorry you didn't like him.'

'Who says I didn't like him?' her friend frowned. 'How could any woman *not* like him?'

'He is rather attractive——'

'He's delicious,' Jenny sighed. 'But I won't have you almost destroying yourself over him again!'

'No, ma'am,' she affected a good imitation of Kyle's attractive drawl.

'Don't be cheeky,' her friend warned. 'That man makes Kenny Whitney look like a mere child when it comes to lethal charm.'

She couldn't help smiling at that apt description of Kyle; she was just surprised she hadn't realised it sooner than she had. 'You've realised that already, have you?' she mused.

'Who could miss it?' Jenny drooled. 'But enough about him, let's get you home.'

'I'll be all right on my own,' Shelby assured her as she stood up to collect her things.

Jenny's mouth opened in protest, and then quickly clamped shut again as she saw Shelby's stubborn expression. 'Go straight to bed as soon as you get home,' she was still issuing orders as Shelby climbed into the waiting taxi.

She smiled up at the other woman. 'I think I'm going to have to do something about you,' she murmured teasingly. 'All this new-found power has gone to your head.'

Jenny grinned. 'And at the moment you aren't strong enough to stop me.'

'But I will be,' she warned half seriously. 'And when I am, watch out!'

'I'm hoping by that time motherhood will have mellowed you,' Jenny mocked.

She laughed softly. 'When you hope to take over running the salon full time.'

'Yes.'

'You've got it all worked out, haven't you?' she couldn't help chuckling.

'You bet,' Jenny grinned.

Shelby's own humour faded as soon as the taxi was out of eyesight of the salon. Kyle was here, actually in London! And she knew that if it weren't for the baby they would have been able to resume their affair for the time he was here. Kyle simply wasn't the type of man to just look up an old mistress, he had obviously intended them to become lovers again.

Three months hadn't dulled her love for him in the least, in fact the baby growing inside her meant it had increased. And she had to deny them both, couldn't do any other.

She was a little annoyed when she got home to find that as well as calling the lawyers for her and cancelling her appointment for this afternoon Jenny had also telephoned her doctor. He arrived a few minutes after she did, giving her a firm reprimand after finding her blood pressure was slightly raised, ordering her to stay away from the salon for another week. She knew Jenny was only doing what she thought best for her, but she cursed the other woman for her interference as she was instructed to go to bed and stay there.

But she would be up and waiting for Kyle when he arrived, she was determined about that . . .

CHAPTER NINE

A LIGHT burnt low on her bedside table when she woke, taking a few minutes to become aware of her surroundings, her eyes widening in shock as she saw the man sitting beside her bed.

'Kyle . . .?' she questioned warily, still not sure that seeing him at all hadn't been a dream.

He sat forward so that the lamp cast his face in a golden shadow. 'Don't be alarmed,' he soothed. 'The maid let me in when I told her who I was.'

She blinked, not imagining Susan letting just anyone into her flat. 'Who you are?' she asked slowly.

He nodded. 'I told her I was a friend. My name seemed to do the trick.'

Because Susan had assumed he was the 'Mr Whitney' she was going to marry! Her maid had never met Kenny, his visits to her flat always made in the evening when the middle-aged woman had gone home for the day.

'What time is it?' she asked sleepily.

'Eight-thirty.'

'Eight——!' She blinked dazedly. She had slept for over six hours. 'I'm sorry, Kyle,' she frowned. 'I had no idea . . . I meant to be up in time for dinner.'

'You will be,' he stood up. 'I'll have it cooked by the time you've showered and dressed.'

She sat up quickly, and then wished she hadn't as the room revolved for several seconds. 'I couldn't ask you to cook dinner——'

'You didn't,' he told her softly, his dark gaze

moving to the thrust of her breasts beneath the black lacy nightgown she wore. 'I offered,' he added gruffly.

She blushed under the heady warmth of his gaze, wishing she could fulfil the promise of passion in his eyes. Instead she chose to ignore it. 'In that case,' she said lightly, 'I accept. Ten minutes?'

He dragged his gaze up to her face with an effort. 'Fine,' he nodded tersely.

She was determined to erase that lapse into intimacy, her dress completely shapeless, although the green was a perfect match for her eyes. She applied only the lightest of make-up, just enough to stop her looking too pale, her mouth outlined in pale peach lipgloss. No one could accuse her of trying to attract Kyle!

He had prepared two beautiful steaks by the time she joined him in the kitchen. His casual glance took in everything about her as he turned from serving up the food, although he made no comment, either derogatory or complimentary, just as she didn't comment on his appearance—dark and virile in casual grey trousers and a black, fitted shirt.

'Is there anything I can do to help?' she asked brightly after finding he already had the table laid.

'The wine is in the 'fridge.' He carried the plates through to the dining-room. 'Sit and eat,' he ordered as she moved about the kitchen tidying up the small amount of mess he had made while he worked.

She sat. His arrogance hadn't changed at all. Thank goodness! She didn't want anything about him to change, loved him just the way he was.

'Why didn't you ever telephone again?' he

asked suddenly after they had been eating in silence for several enjoyable minutes.

She looked up in surprise, frowning slightly as she sensed reprimand. 'Telephone . . .?'

He nodded, his eyes narrowed. 'The ranch. I expected you to call back after Helen told you I wasn't at home. But you never did.'

Too much had happened since that time for her to dare call him again. She moistened dry lips. 'Didn't Helen give you my message? She said she would.'

'She gave it to me,' he acknowledged grimly. 'I still expected you to call back.'

'Why?'

'Damn it, because——' he broke off, drawing in a controlling breath. 'Didn't our time together mean anything to you?' he demanded bitterly. 'Or was I just another good time to you, a salve to your pride after Kenny decided not to marry you?'

Her eyes gleamed angrily. 'That's a foul thing to say!'

'But true?'

'You know it isn't,' she snapped. 'I was always honest with you about my attraction to you.'

'Then why the silence after you left?' he bit out. 'Do you have any idea how I felt having to ask Kenny for your address?'

She could imagine it only too well, she could also imagine Kenny's pleasure in being the one to have the information Kyle needed. He surely wouldn't have made it easy, especially as he would rather the two of them never met again. 'I never imagined you would want it,' she shrugged. 'As for telephoning again,' she added hardly, 'I could never be sure you wouldn't be out visiting Mrs Judd.'

His eyes narrowed to steely slits at her sarcasm. 'I told you, she's only a friend.'

'So you did.' She continued to eat, although she was no longer enjoying the delicious food, just needing something to do. She and Kyle were behaving like jealous lovers, and although they had assuredly been the latter you had to feel love to know the former. And Kyle didn't love her. Maybe he was just annoyed at the fact that he didn't have the willing lover waiting for him in London that he had envisaged. 'How are Kenny and Wendy?' she changed the subject abruptly.

'They've moved in with Wendy's father now,' Kyle answered after a slight hesitation.

'He's forgiven them, then.'

'Yes. He——' he sighed. 'The advent of his first grandchild did the trick,' he revealed curtly.

'Wendy's pregnant?' her eyes widened. 'How wonderful for them.'

'You think so?' he said dryly.

'Don't you?' she frowned.

'I was thinking of you.'

'Me?' She expressed her surprise.

'It could have been your child if you had married Kenny as planned,' he rasped.

The thought of the child she carried being Kenny's filled her with revulsion. She moistened her lips as they became dry again. 'What a lucky escape I had!'

'You don't want children?'

'I don't want Kenny's children,' she shuddered. 'How has he taken to the idea of fatherhood?' she added quickly before he could ask if she would mind someone else fathering her child.

Kyle's mouth twisted. 'He would like anything if it meant it bridged the rift with Ben.'

'That's cynical,' she reprimanded gently. 'He might make a good father.'

'As his own was!' he rasped.

'He can't be held responsible for his father's actions,' she pointed out reasoningly.

Kyle became suddenly still. 'You know about that?'

'Helen told me,' she nodded. 'It may not all have been her husband's fault, the woman involved must have encouraged him to a certain degree.'

'Oh she did,' he acknowledged grimly. 'The woman involved was my mother!'

Shelby was left speechless. Katherine had been *Kyle's* mother! It was incredible, tragic—and it explained so many things, Helen's gratitude that she had been allowed to stay on at the ranch even after her husband's betrayal of his family, Kenny's resentment of both Kyle and his father over what he considered to be their charity.

'Tell me about it,' she encouraged softly.

He was scowling heavily, having imbibed more than his share of the wine after Shelby had refused more than one glass. 'I thought you said you knew about it.'

'Only that Helen's husband left her for another woman, I had no idea it was your mother.'

He shrugged. 'There isn't much more than that to tell. My uncle's and my mother's selfish love for each other left two families broken-hearted.'

'From what Helen told me of her husband she was better off without him!'

His eyes were icy. 'Maybe she was, but my father never got over my mother's desertion of us. He died when I was only twenty. Can you imagine that, a man of forty-eight just giving up and dying?'

'He must have loved her very much,' Shelby sympathised.

'Yes,' Kyle ground out.

'And your uncle and mother?' she prompted.

'They were married after the divorces. I expec they're still together somewhere.'

'Don't you know?' she gasped.

Kyle glared at her. 'I don't *want* to know!'

'I'm sorry,' she told him quietly. 'I didn' mean to interfere. I suppose it's just that both my own parents being dead made me think it wa better to have one parent alive than none.'

'My mother has what she wanted,' he bit out 'She didn't give a damn about either of us when she walked out. And I'll never forgive her fo killing my father.'

The cold set to his face told her that he neve would either. Kyle was a man of deep and lasting feelings, and the woman who had mothered him would never know his forgiveness.

But as he had spoken of his mother and uncle something else had occurred to her, something that she didn't even want to contemplate bu which persisted in tormenting her.

'What about me, Kyle?' she suddenly asked jerkily, unable to contain herself any longer.

He looked at her with narrowed grey eyes 'What about you?'

'Where did I fit into the scheme of things? Wa I a salve to *your* ego?' She looked at him unblinkingly. 'You accused me of using you, bu couldn't it have been the other way around?'

'What the hell are you talking about?' he rasped impatiently.

'A little old-fashioned retribution—twenty-two years too late. Did the fact that I wa supposed to be Kenny's wife make me more attractive to you?' She was breathing hard in her agitation.

'Don't be ridiculous——'

'Am I being?' she derided. 'You despised me from the moment you met me, before then even, and yet in the end you had an affair with me!'

'Because I wanted you!'

'Was it?' her voice was shrill. 'Or was it because one day you might have had the pleasure of telling Kenny you slept with his ex-fiancé?'

Kyle was so stony-faced now he looked as if he were carved from granite. 'You can't really believe what you're saying,' he grated.

'I don't want to——'

'But you do anyway,' he pushed back his chair to stand up. 'I think I'd better go,' he bit out abruptly. 'We've obviously got nothing more to say to each other.'

'Kyle!' She turned anxiously to stop him as he reached the door.

He was pulling on his thick outdoor coat. 'It's better if I leave,' he repeated tautly.

She could see him leaving her life once again, this time angrily, with no chance of him ever coming back, and she couldn't let him do it. 'Kyle, don't go!' She stood up to rush across the room towards him, her arms going about his waist beneath his coat, her face pressed against the firm wall of his chest. 'Don't go,' she repeated raggedly, her lashes tear-wet as she looked up at him with pleading eyes.

For long agonising moments he continued to look down at her with hard uncompromising eyes, then he gave a muffled groan as his arms came about her and he buried his face in her hair.

'I'm sorry, so sorry,' she murmured between

kisses, neither of them seeming able to ge
enough of each other.

'Forget it,' he dismissed. 'God, how I've
wanted this!' His arms tightened about her.

It was too late to put a stop to this even if she
wanted to, she knew that even as their mouth
fused in an earth-shattering kiss that left them
both breathless and wanting more. She would
have to take the risk of Kyle discovering the
changes in her body because she just didn't have
the strength to deny him or herself.

His eyes were dark as he looked down at her
'It is what you want too?' He kept a check on his
desire as he waited for her answer.

Now was the time to say no, now was the time
for her to retreat from any further physica
contact with him. But even as she thought that
her body melted against his. 'Yes,' she breathed
'It's what I want too.'

'Thank God for that,' he groaned. 'You've
been so damned distant since I arrived at the
salon this afternoon that it's been like being with
a stranger.'

'It's been almost three months, Kyle, I was a
little shy with you.'

'Is that really what it was?'

'Take me to bed, Kyle,' she encouraged
throatily. 'Make love to me.'

'I intend to, until you beg for mercy,' he
promised.

They undressed each other heatedly once they
reached her bedroom, eager for the feel and touch
of each other, falling on to the bed in a tangle o
arms and legs and questing mouths.

'You're more beautiful than ever,' Kyle told
her gruffly as he cupped the weight of her breas
in his hand, his warm lips moving moistly over

the throbbing tip to suckle and gently bite on the sensitive nipple.

Shelby had heard that a woman's sexual pleasure was often heightened during the middle months of pregnancy, and she knew it was true of herself as spasms of pleasure began to wrack her body at his slightest touch. The pleasure exploded within her as Kyle's hand curved possessively over the warmth of her womanhood, and she buried her face against the pillow in her embarrassment.

Kyle's smile of satisfaction turned to one of concern as he saw the dismay on her face, moving up the bed to lay his head on the pillow next to hers. 'I've missed you too,' he told her throatily. 'In fact I've thought about making love to you for so long that I don't have any control left either!'

And that, coming from a man who was always in control, was an admission indeed. 'Has there been anyone else since——' she broke off, knowing that she should never have asked such a question. Kyle would either have to lie and say no, or tell the truth and hurt her unbearably. 'I'm sorry. Please don't——'

'There's been no one, Shelby,' he answered with such quiet sincerity she couldn't possibly have doubted him. 'You?'

'No,' she shook her head. 'Couldn't you tell?' she added self-derisively.

'Pleasuring your body is more important to me than any I know myself,' he assured her softly.

It was true that he had always been an unselfish lover, but even so she was a little shocked at her own quick response to what had been an exploratory caress. But her response continued through the night as Kyle claimed her again and again, held securely in his arms during moments of rest.

She awoke with the knowledge that Kyle knew nothing of their baby, that all of her fears had been for nothing. The only comment he had made was that she seemed to have put on a little weight, and he found that even more attractive. He slept on as she got out of bed, and remembering her own tiredness from the flight from America she sympathised with him, would have breakfast waiting for him when he did wake.

She had the coffee percolating and the bacon sizzling under the grill when Kyle came into the kitchen fifteen minutes later, only a light robe pulled on over her nakedness while he was fully dressed.

She looked at him shyly. 'So "His Majesty" has deigned to get up, has he?' she mocked him with the same words he had used to her so long ago.

His face relaxed into a smile as he pulled her into his arms to kiss her, his eyes languorous with satisfaction. 'Jet-lag,' he murmured against her lips.

'No excuse,' she teased.

'No,' he grinned down at her. 'I was a little unfair to you then, wasn't I?'

'More than a little!'

'All right, more than a little,' he sighed. 'By the way,' he added conversationally, 'I think the bacon is burning.'

'Oh no!' She turned to pull out the grill-pan, finding it was only a little crisper than she usually liked it. 'Go and sit in the other room while I finish cooking breakfast,' she instructed, knowing she wouldn't get anything done in his disturbing presence.

'I'd rather have a shave,' he touched the roughness of his chin ruefully. 'I couldn't see a razor in the bathroom.'

'Top drawer of the dressing-table,' she told him in a preoccupied voice. 'It's an electric one.'

'I could always grow a beard!'

'No, you were right at the cabin, it doesn't suit you,' she told him cheekily. 'Besides, my skin is too delicate to be scraped again while you grow it.'

'Top drawer you said,' he derided.

She hummed to herself as she finished cooking, cherishing the fact that he hadn't denied being about long enough to grow a beard. Once again she was going to take what time she could with him, would face the heartache all over again once he had gone back to Montana.

'Who's this?'

She turned at Kyle's rasping query, almost dropping the plates in her hand as she saw the photograph he held. She had forgotten pushing the photograph of Gavin in the top drawer of her dressing-table before leaving the bedroom this morning, knowing that if Kyle saw it he was sure to ask questions, and now he was doing exactly that.

Her expression remained bland as she carried the plates through to the dining-room. 'It's my husband, of course,' she answered lightly.

Kyle looked down at the photograph with narrowed eyes, and Shelby could see exactly what was going through his mind. He would see a good-looking man with greying blond hair and a lithe body, but a man obviously well into middle-age.

His expression was guarded as he looked up at her again. 'This man was your husband?'

'Yes,' she answered defensively. 'Your breakfast is getting cold,' she prompted.

He ignored the latter comment. 'He looks as if he were a lot older than you.'

She nodded. 'He was.'

'And from the salon, rich?'

She drew in a deep breath of resignation as she knew he was about to jump to the conclusion about her marriage that Kenny had been so certain he would. 'Yes,' she acknowledged huskily. 'He was very rich.'

'I see,' he bit out.

She looked up at him with angry eyes, eyes that sparkled like emeralds. 'What exactly do you see, Kyle?' she sighed resignedly.

'I'm sure you know,' he rasped, putting the photograph down with a clatter.

'Yes, I know,' she said bitterly. 'And I'm not even allowed to defend myself, am I? Kenny said——'

'Kenny?' he echoed sharply. 'What does he have to do with this?'

Her mouth twisted. 'Let's just say that your cousin knows you very well and leave it at that. I'm not about to explain myself or my marriage to you. Maybe once I would have tried, but not any more.' Not when he could then turn around and accuse her of using her pregnancy to trap *him* into marriage!

'You don't care enough, is that it?' he grated.

'Care?' she repeated scathingly. 'When did such an emotion enter our relationship?'

'Obviously it didn't,' he snapped.

'Enjoy the time we have together was the way you put it,' she reminded tightly.

'And I have,' he bit out.

'Have?' she echoed hoarsely.

'It's over,' he shrugged. 'Even in an affair there has to be a certain amount of honesty. Would you ever have told me about your husband if I hadn't accidentally seen that photograph?'

'There was nothing to tell,' she said stubbornly. 'And there still isn't.'

'You think so?' he rasped contemptuously. 'I don't happen to agree with you.'

'Gavin was a different part of my life, a part you have no right to judge when you don't know the——'

'Gavin?' he suddenly echoed sharply. '*Gavin* O'Neal was your husband?'

She flushed. 'You've heard of him?' It was a possibility, a very good one, that she hadn't even considered.

'I don't think there can be many people who haven't,' he said bitterly. 'God, woman, he was a legend in the business world.'

'And I was his wife,' she nodded.

Kyle shook his head dazedly. 'It's amazing.'

'What is?' she asked warily.

'That you were going to marry Kenny after being with a man like that!'

'I only marry for love,' she told him stiffly. 'And for a time I thought I loved Kenny.'

'And what do you go to bed for?' Kyle asked contemptuously.

She breathed deeply at the insult. 'Pleasure!' she snapped resentfully. 'What about you?'

'The same,' he rasped. 'And this has just stopped being that. I'm no more willing to become a rich widow's plaything than Kenny was. At least he came to his senses enough to realise that!'

'His decision not to marry me had nothing to do with sense,' she flared.

'What do you mean?' His eyes were narrowed.

'Ask Kenny,' she dismissed. 'And if by some miracle he should actually tell you the truth, don't come back to me with apologies,' she bit out forcefully.

'Apologies?' he questioned disbelievingly.

'Yes,' she snapped. 'And I won't be interested in hearing them!'

'I'll never make them!'

She didn't cry once he had left, didn't feel anything. Last night had been an illusion, a beautiful one, and that was all she wanted to remember of Kyle's visit to London.

CHAPTER TEN

DESPITE the doctor's instructions she knew she couldn't stay in her flat all day, knowing that today of all days it would do more harm than good, that she would only brood about the way she and Kyle had parted. Telephoning Gavin's lawyer she made arrangements to see him later that morning.

'It's very unusual,' Hugh Prewitt frowned at her suggestion as he sat across the desk from her.

'So are the circumstances, surely?' she mused, knowing she had shocked the poor man a few minutes ago when she had told him of her condition. An elderly man with kind brown eyes he had been good to her both before and after Gavin's death, and what she was telling him now must be a little disturbing to him.

He cleared his throat noisily. 'I suppose they are,' he acknowledged. 'But Mr O'Neal's will didn't cover such a contingency.'

'I'm not surprised,' she said self-derisively. 'All I want to know is, can it be done?'

'Well of course. But——'

'Then do it,' she told him firmly, knowing this was what she wanted.

'Have you thought about this properly?' the lawyer prompted softly. 'Considered everything carefully?'

'Everything,' she nodded. 'Gavin loved me and I loved him, but I certainly don't expect him to support another man's child.'

'But transferring the money back to his sisters

will be an irreversible process that you may one day regret.'

'I don't think so, Hugh,' she assured him gently, realising how upsetting this must be for him. 'I may not be getting married, but I will have my own family, and I can't expect Gavin's money to support that family.'

'I'm sure he——'

'I know,' she acknowledged quietly. 'Gavin wouldn't have minded. But I do.'

'You intend to seek support from the child's father?'

'No!'

The lawyer frowned again. 'Under English law you are entitled to——'

'Claiming support means giving the father rights I don't intend him to have,' she dismissed hardly. 'Besides, I don't need it.'

'Not at this moment in time, no,' he agreed. 'But one day perhaps——'

'If that day ever comes then I'll do something about it. In the meantime I want you to return all Gavin's money to his sisters. That should please them, I'm sure,' she added dryly.

'Perhaps. But as your adviser in this I have to tell you that I feel strongly——'

'Thank you for your concern, Hugh,' she smiled. 'But my mind is made up.'

'I can see that,' he sighed. 'Then all I can do is wish you good luck for the future. I hope everything turns out as you would wish it to.'

So did she. Although now that she had disposed of Gavin's fortune she felt as if at least part of the weight had been lifted from her shoulders. She had known for some time that she would have to make that move, it had just been a question of getting in to see Hugh and putting the wheels in motion.

While she had been just Gavin's widow she had felt legally bound by his will to at least keep the money in her bank account even if she hadn't touched a penny of it. But as the mother of Kyle's child the situation changed drastically. And neither she nor the baby would starve on the profit made from the salon.

'And just what do you think you're doing here?' Jenny demanded when she walked into the salon after lunch.

Shelby gave her a serene untroubled smile. 'I've come to check up on my business.'

'You should be home in bed!'

'Now there's a thought,' she mocked.

'Shelby——'

'Jenny!' She gave her friend a pointed look, the teasing gone momentarily.

The other woman sighed. 'Well at least sit down.' She encouraged Shelby to occupy one of the plush armchairs that were scattered about the salon.

'I'd rather stand,' she refused. 'How's business today?'

'Booming, as usual. Shelby, don't you think——'

'No, I don't,' she answered firmly. 'I need to keep busy today, and this seems as good a place as any.'

Jenny frowned. 'Dinner didn't go well last night?'

'It was breakfast this morning that didn't go well,' she dismissed.

'Oh? Oh!' Jenny said again as realisation dawned. 'Should you be doing that sort of thing in your condition?'

'Why not?' she mocked. 'It was doing "that sort of thing" that got me into *this* condition!'

'I must say, you seem in a good mood.' Jenny looked worried.

'A good night of lust and debauchery is apt to have that effect on me,' she teased.

'Shelby!' Jenny looked about them self-consciously, the salon full to capacity as usual, several people sitting close enough to hear their conversation.

She laughed softly. 'Don't look so shocked,' she smiled. 'I'm told everyone does it.'

'But not everyone talks about it in such a public place.' Jenny hustled her to the back of the salon and into her office. 'If you want something to do then sit behind your desk and look beautiful,' she said firmly.

The paperwork she had left on her desk the day before kept her occupied for the rest of the afternoon, not giving her time to think of the fact that Kyle was probably concluding his business as quickly as possible so that he might return to Montana.

It was late afternoon when she heard the sound of raised voices coming from the salon, getting up at once to find out what was going on. She met one of her manicurists outside. 'What's happening?' she demanded to know.

'He came into the salon a few minutes ago, and when Jenny tried to get him to leave he started ranting and raving——'

'He?' Shelby groaned. It just wasn't their week! Her customers certainly wouldn't appreciate a man seeing them in some of the preparation it took for them to keep their looks. And this one sounded as if he might actually *be* drunk.

'Jenny's trying to calm him down,' Sally looked worried. 'But without much effect.'

Shelby could tell that as the raised voices continued to be heard, hurrying outside to try and stop the noise herself. The scene that met her eyes stopped her in her tracks. Kyle stood just inside the salon, a disreputable bunch of flowers in his hand, his face flushed as he and Jenny shouted at each other across the room.

'Kyle?' she spoke loud enough to be heard.

He turned glazed eyes on her, swaying slightly. 'I knew you were here. *She*,' he looked accusingly at Jenny, 'tried to tell me you weren't.'

Shelby's eyes widened as she realised something. 'You're drunk,' she gasped.

'That's what I've been trying to tell him,' Jenny cut in angrily.

'I don't need telling,' he snapped. 'I know exactly what I am.'

'I was only trying to stop him coming through and upsetting you,' Jenny looked at her pleadingly.

She nodded, not taking her eyes off Kyle, so bemused by seeing him in this state that she didn't quite know what to say. She needn't have worried about that, Kyle had plenty to say for all of them!

'I didn't intend upsetting her,' he bit out with the preciseness of a person who has had too much to drink. 'I came to bring her these,' he held up the flowers, several of the stems bent or actually broken. 'Oh,' he frowned down at them. 'I must have sat on them in the cab,' he murmured dazedly.

'They're lovely, Kyle,' she hurried forward to take the flowers from him. 'Thank you.'

'That isn't all,' he spoke loudly. 'I came to tell you that I don't care if you're the richest woman in the world, I want to be your—your consort.'

She stopped trying to pull him to the privacy of the office, looking up at him dazedly. Had he really said what she thought he had. 'Kyle . . .?'

'I want to marry you,' the grey eyes were suddenly focused on her with deep intensity. 'I came to London with the intention of doing just that,' his voice had lowered now, the enormity of his declaration seeming to have sobered him somewhat. 'I love you, Shelby. Will you marry me?'

'Yes,' she answered without hesitation.

He looked taken aback. 'Really?'

'Really,' she nodded.

'I don't want any of your money, you know,' he told her as several of the people closest to them began to clap, having heard the proposal.

'As of this morning there isn't that much money,' she assured him as they moved towards the back of the salon.

He frowned his puzzlement. 'There isn't?'

'No,' she smiled.

'Did you spend it all?' he asked indulgently.

Her smile widened. 'Not quite,' she drawled. 'Jenny could you get us some coffee, please? Black,' she added pointedly.

'With pleasure,' Jenny nodded, closing the office door firmly behind them.

'She doesn't like me,' Kyle muttered as he almost fell on to the sofa, his eyes closed.

'She doesn't know you,' Shelby told him soothingly, taking off his shoes before putting his feet up on the sofa to make him more comfortable.

He grimaced. 'Meaning she'll love me when she does.'

Shelby sat back on her haunches. 'I didn't say that . . .'

'My head aches,' he groaned, a hand over his eyes.

'Just relax,' she soothed again.

'We have to talk——'

'We can do that later,' she quietened him. 'Just lie back and rest.'

He was fast asleep by the time Jenny arrived with the tray of coffee, Shelby inviting her inside anyway.

'I think we're the ones who could do with the coffee,' she said ruefully as she poured two cups.

Jenny looked over at the sleeping man, his face still flushed from the alcohol he had consumed. 'Are you really going to marry him?' she murmured.

Shelby nodded. 'If he asks me again when he's sober.' And that was something she wasn't sure he would do. The mere fact that he was drunk was completely out of character for him, so his proposal could be too, something he would deeply regret when he sobered up.

'Do you think he will?' Jenny quietly echoed her troubled thoughts.

'I don't know. But I hope so.'

'The salon is buzzing with talk of his proposal, and everyone wants to know who he is.'

'He certainly livened the place up,' she agreed ruefully.

'That's one way of putting it,' her friend agreed dryly. 'Do you intend going back to Montana with him if he does repeat his offer of marriage?'

'If he does repeat it, yes,' she nodded unhesitatingly. 'After all, I have a very able assistant who is more than capable of managing things for me here.'

'That's true,' Jenny smiled, standing up.

'How long do you think it will be before he wakes up?'

They both looked over at the sleeping Kyle, Shelby's heart contracting painfully at how vulnerable he looked, his face flushed, his hair falling untidily across his forehead. 'Anyone's guess,' she grimaced. 'I'm sure this must be a first for him.'

'The proposal or the drunkenness?'

'Both!'

The afternoon passed into early evening, and still Kyle slept on. Not that Shelby minded that, she wanted him stone-cold sober when he did wake up. She needed to know exactly what had prompted him to come to the salon this afternoon. Had he telephoned Kenny and found out the truth, or had he come to see her anyway, still believing her to be a rich widow? Not that she thought for a moment that he was interested in the money, she knew him well enough to be sure of that, but she still wondered how he was going to react when she told him what she had done. And there was also the baby to explain. She was unsure of his reaction to that too!

'I'm off now,' Jenny came in to tell her just after six. 'Everything is locked up.'

'Thanks,' she nodded.

Jenny raised blonde eyebrows at the still-sleeping man. 'Shouldn't you wake him?'

The truth of it was that she was reluctant to do so. While he slept she could cling to the fact that he had told her he loved her and asked her to marry her. But she knew that a wide-awake, sober Kyle could regret and retract every word he had said.

The sound of their voices seemed to have penetrated his sleep, and he stirred restlessly.

'I'll see you tomorrow,' Jenny said, making a quick departure.

Shelby could understand her haste to be gone after the slanging match she had had with Kyle earlier; she was more than a little uncertain herself what sort of mood he was going to be in when he did wake up.

'God . . .!' he groaned weakly as he tried to sit up, pushing back the coat she had draped over him. He looked about him dazedly, his face pale now as he focused on Shelby sitting across the room from him, the desk-lamp their only illumination. 'Shelby?' he questioned slowly.

She didn't get up, feeling more confident behind the desk. 'How do you feel?'

'Awful!' He rubbed his aching temples, suddenly looking up at her frowningly. 'And as if I made a bloody fool of myself,' he added questioningly.

Her expression softened. 'Everyone is entitled to one drunken binge in their lifetime.'

He winced as she didn't refute his claim. 'Not here, and in front of all those people.'

'"Those people" enjoyed the floor-show immensely!'

Kyle grimaced at the description. 'And how about you, did you enjoy it too?'

He seemed almost wary, and her own reply was just as guarded. 'It was—interesting.'

'I'll bet it was,' he muttered, swinging his legs to the floor as he sat round, his elbows resting on his knees as he cradled his aching head in his hands. 'What did I say?'

'You don't remember?' she delayed.

'I—God, yes,' he moaned as it all came back to him. 'I must have embarrassed the hell out of you!'

She shook her head. 'Not really.'

'How not really?' he looked at her with narrowed eyes.

She shrugged. 'I was so surprised to see you—like that, that I didn't really feel anything else.'

'Not even when I asked you to marry me?' he rasped.

The colour darkened her cheeks. 'That surprised me most of all.'

Kyle stood up, moving restlessly about the room, frowning as he looked out of the window. 'What time is it?'

'About six-thirty.'

'How long was I out?'

'Three hours or so,' she shrugged.

'No wonder I have a headache,' he bit out. 'Well headache or not, we have to talk. I meant everything I said to you this afternoon,' he looked at her intently.

'Can you remember exactly what you did say?' she asked guardedly.

'Yes,' he still held her gaze. 'I do love you, and I want to marry you.'

Her breath left her body in a relieved sigh. 'Then you must remember my answer,' she said huskily.

He nodded. 'But I'd still like to hear it again.'

She chewed on her bottom lip for several minutes, not answering him. 'Did you talk to Kenny after you left here this morning?'

'Kenny?' he asked dazedly. 'What does he have to do with this?'

'Did you?' she persisted.

'No, I didn't,' he answered impatiently. 'And I don't intend to either. Shelby, I stayed in Montana for almost three months after you left me, if I had wanted to talk to him I would have done so then. I'm not interested in anything he has to tell me.'

'I didn't leave you,' she corrected. 'I came home.'

'It amounts to the same thing,' he dismissed.

'Not at all. If you had once asked me to stay I would have done.'

'Even then?'

'Even then,' she nodded.

'Then I wish to God I had, because the time I've been without you has been pure hell,' he bit out.

'It's been the same for me.'

'You love me?'

'I have for some time,' she confirmed huskily. 'I realised it when you came back from looking for Kenny and Wendy. I would never have had an affair with you if I hadn't.'

Kyle came round the desk to pull her effortlessly into his arms. 'Will you marry me?'

Curved against the hardness of his body as she was it was difficult not to fling herself into his arms and tell him that of course she would marry him. But they still had so much to talk about before she could commit herself.

She pulled out of his arms, moving a short distance away. 'I have to talk to you about Gavin before I answer that question——'

'I don't give a damn about your first husband,' he dismissed with his usual impatience. 'Oh I know I reacted badly this morning, that I even got drunk because of it, but it did come as a shock to realise just how rich you are.'

'Were you hoping to bribe me into marriage with the ranch as bait?' she mocked.

'If I had to,' he admitted grimly. 'It threw me when I got here yesterday and realised you owned this place, finding out you were Gavin O'Neal's widow made me realise you didn't need me for anything.'

'But I do,' she contradicted earnestly. 'I need you very badly. But there are some things about Gavin and myself that I think you should be aware of.'

'Then tell me,' he encouraged softly.

She did so, haltingly at first, and then more quickly, as if to get it over and done with. 'So you see,' she concluded breathlessly, 'if I marry again I forfeit Gavin's money.' She looked at him intently.

'Which is why Kenny changed his mind about marrying you,' Kyle realised grimly.

His astuteness warmed her. 'Yes,' she nodded. 'Although if you asked him he was going to tell you *I* changed my mind because I found out he didn't own half the Double K. He told me he did, you see,' she explained at Kyle's puzzled expression.

'When did he threaten you with that?' he rasped.

'When he got back from Las Vegas and realised something had happened between us.'

'A black eye was too lenient,' Kyle bit out furiously. 'I'll kill him when I get back!'

She shrugged. 'As long as you believe that I didn't just think I was marrying another rich man it isn't important.' She looked at him uncertainly.

'Shelby, one thing I learnt about you in Montana, and that I was blind to this morning, is that you're scrupulously honest,' he told her gently. 'I'm sure you wouldn't have married Kenny for any other reason than that you thought you loved him. God, you were giving up a fortune to marry the young idiot,' he rasped disgustedly. 'He didn't realise how lucky he would have been! Will you mind giving it up to marry me, because I can't settle for anything less than a lifetime commitment from you?'

'I've already given it up.'

He frowned. 'You have?'

'Kyle, when did you know you loved me?'

'What does that have to do——'

'Just tell me,' she encouraged throatily. 'It's important.'

For a moment he just continued to look at her, and then he shrugged. 'At the cabin,' he answered bluntly. 'Away from the ranch you didn't seem to be the woman Kenny had described. I found myself liking you in spite of myself. The snowball fight we had was the most lighthearted fun I'd had in years,' his expression softened, 'and I could tell you enjoyed it too. But I didn't want to make love to you, felt as if I was taking advantage of the situation and you. But when I saw you naked in front of the fire that night I couldn't stop myself. And it was the most erotic and beautiful experience of my life.'

That was what Shelby had wanted to know, what she had most wanted to hear!

'Until the next day when I realised I had made love to a very sick woman,' he added hardly.

'It wasn't like that!'

'It was,' he insisted flatly.

'It wasn't,' she went to him then, her arms up about his neck. 'I knew exactly what I was doing, that night, and when you came back from Las Vegas.'

His arms tightened about her. 'You'll never know how much it cost me to let you leave after the time we had shared together.'

'You seemed cheerful at the airport,' she accused with remembered pain.

'Only because you did. You seemed to want to go home,' he said gruffly. 'And after all that had happened I had no right to try and stop you.'

'You had the best right in the world,' her lips caressed his jaw. 'Kyle, when do Kenny and Wendy expect their baby?' she murmured against his throat.

'Just before Christmas,' he answered in a puzzled voice. 'But what——'

'Then you're going to be a father first,' she told him softly.

He was justifiably startled. 'A father?' His gaze moved questioningly over her stomach. 'I thought there was something different about you . . .!'

'And I thought you hadn't cared enough to notice,' she pouted up at him.

'I noticed. But I— Is this the reason you're giving up your husband's money?' he frowned.

'I haven't given up anything,' she chided softly. 'Because I never considered it mine in the first place.' She explained how she hadn't touched a penny of the money since Gavin died. 'And I'm so glad you feel the way you do about our time at the cabin, because that's when our baby was conceived.'

'Could it be any other way?' he groaned gruffly, kissing her with a gentleness that bordered on reverence.

'You don't mind that we're going to have a family straight away?' she voiced her last doubt when she could get her breath.

He shook his head, a deep glow in his eyes. 'I'd like four or five girls—and all of them just like their mother.'

She smiled her relief. 'I think you could be biased.'

'One hundred per cent!' he agreed huskily before he began to kiss her again and they forgot everything but the present moment.

Enter a uniquely exciting new world with

Harlequin American Romance™·

Harlequin American Romances are the first romances to explore today's love relationships. These compelling novels reach into the hearts and minds of women across America... probing the most intimate moments of romance, love and desire.

You'll follow romantic heroines and irresistible men as they boldly face confusing choices. Career first, love later? Love without marriage? Long-distance relationships? All the experiences that make love real are captured in the tender, loving pages of **Harlequin American Romances.**

What makes American women so different when it comes to love? Find out with **Harlequin American Romance!**

Send for your introductory FREE book now!

Get this book FREE!

Harlequin American Romance

Twice in a Lifetime
REBECCA FLANDERS

Mail to:
Harlequin Reader Service

In the U.S.
2504 West Southern Ave.
Tempe, AZ 85282

In Canada
P.O. Box 2800, Postal Station A
5170 Yonge St., Willowdale, Ont. M2N 5T5

YES! I want to be one of the first to discover
Harlequin American Romance. Send me FREE and without
obligation *Twice in a Lifetime.* If you do not hear from me after I
have examined my FREE book, please send me the 4 new
Harlequin American Romances each month as soon as they
come off the presses. I understand that I will be billed only $2.25
for each book (total $9.00). There are no shipping or handling
charges. There is no minimum number of books that I have to
purchase. In fact, I may cancel this arrangement at any time.
Twice in a Lifetime is mine to keep as a FREE gift, even if I do not
buy any additional books. 154 BPA NAZJ

Name   (please print)

Address   Apt. no.

City   State/Prov.   Zip/Postal Code

Signature (If under 18, parent or guardian must sign.)

This offer is limited to one order per household and not valid to current Harlequin
American Romance subscribers. We reserve the right to exercise discretion in
granting membership. If price changes are necessary, you will be notified.

AMR-SUB-3

Readers rave about Harlequin American Romance!

"...the best series of modern romances I have read...great, exciting, stupendous, wonderful."
—S.E.*, Coweta, Oklahoma

"...they are absolutely fantastic...going to be a smash hit and hard to keep on the bookshelves."
—P.D., Easton, Pennsylvania

"The American line is great. I've enjoyed every one I've read so far."
—W.M.K., Lansing, Illinois

"...the best stories I have read in a long time."
—R.H., Northport, New York

*Names available on request.